JILLIAN HART

KLONDIKE HERO

Steeple
Hill®

Published by Steeple Hill Books™

Special thanks and acknowledgment to Jillian Hart for her contribution to the ALASKAN BRIDE RUSH miniseries

STEEPLE HILL BOOKS

Steeple
Hill®

Recycling programs
for this product may
not exist in your area.

ISBN-13: 978-0-373-87608-2

KLONDIKE HERO

Copyright © 2010 by Harlequin Books S.A.

www.SteepleHill.com

Printed in U.S.A.

"Why don't you like me, Gage?"

She hitched her chin up a notch, studying him with blue eyes capable of bending unsuspecting men to her will.

"As far as I can tell, Karenna, you ran out on your wedding. What you're doing here in a wedding dress is anyone's guess. Why didn't you change on the way? Or did you think the men here would be rubes, easily tricked into marrying you, so you didn't bother to change?"

"Believe me, if you are anything like the rest of the men in this town, then I want to sue that magazine for false reporting. You are hardly hunky, marriage-minded or charming." Okay, maybe she'd gotten carried away. Gage Parker *was* hunky, but that was about all the good she could say about him.

Alaskan Bride Rush: Women are flocking to the Land of the Midnight Sun with marriage on their minds

JILLIAN HART

grew up on her family's homestead, where she helped raise cattle, rode horses and scribbled stories in her spare time. After earning her English degree from Whitman College, she worked in travel and advertising before selling her first novel. When Jillian isn't working on her next story, she can be found puttering in her rose garden, curled up with a good book or spending quiet evenings at home with her family.

The Lord is near to all who call upon Him.
—*Psalms* 145:18

Prologue

Karenna Digby pulled her car in front of the diner in nowhere, Washington State—she had no idea where she was—and grabbed her purse from the passenger seat. The lace cuff of her sleeve caught on the emergency brake. Stupid wedding dress. She was tired, heartbroken and starving. She couldn't remember when she'd last had a real meal, since she'd been dieting to fit into her gown for months.

She shoved open the door, the tap of rain on her face felt like the tears she could not shed. She grabbed her purse and her dress's train, planted her expensive white shoes on either side of a huge puddle. Yes, she *would* have to park in a puddle. That was the way her day—her would-be wedding day—was going. She slammed the door and spotted the "Just Married" sign on her back window.

Stupid sign. She skirted the puddle, tossed her train over the crook of her arm and tore at it. It ripped in half, one piece sticking stubbornly to the window. What had her sisters used to adhere it to the glass? Superpowered glue? It wouldn't come off.

The heavens opened, and the rain turned to a torrential downpour. Leaving the tattered half of the sign for later, she wove around the puddles on the worn blacktop. She could only hope she didn't look as bedraggled as she felt—then she caught her reflection in the diner's windows and groaned at the lonely bride with wilting roses braided into her hair.

"Table for two?" The gum-cracking waitress asked at the rickety podium that served as a hostess stand.

"No. There's just me."

"I see. Sorry to hear it. Once that happened to me, too, honey." She led the way down the aisle in sensible rubber shoes that squeaked with her gait. "What you have to do is not let it get to you. Get back up, shake off the hurt and find you another man. Don't let one bad seed ruin your attitude about love."

"Thanks." She slipped into the booth patched with duct tape and let the train fall to the bench beside her. At least she wasn't the only bride in history to have been left at the altar. It just felt that way.

"Menus are on the table." The waitress pulled a pad out of her pocket. "What you want to drink, hon?"

"Coffee, please." She would start with that. Her stomach might be growling, but she wasn't sure she could keep down anything more than liquids. Devastation hung on her like a lead weight. She thought of her family's fury at her, and her younger sisters, both married of course, patting her consolingly. "He'll come to his senses," Kim had said. "You just have to be patient with him," Katie had advised.

Patient? She wanted to be married. She had the dress. She'd had the groom. She had a future as Alan's wife all mapped out. How could he do this to her? Her two-carat engagement ring sparkled as she reached for the worn, laminated menus tucked between the paper napkin dispenser and the wall. She didn't know what to do. She'd dated Alan for seven years. They'd been high-school sweethearts and attended the University of Washington together, strolling hand in hand down the tree-lined avenues and along picturesque walkways, and studying in their favorite carrels in the undergraduate library.

Now that was all gone. All the love and hope vanished as if they'd never been.

Send me a sign, Lord. Please. Show me what to do. She yanked the menu free, and bold print caught her eye. There was a magazine tucked against the wall, its pages folded over to an article with a catchy headline. "Treasure Creek, Alaska, Seeks Brides for Hunky Habitants!" Rain dripped off her hair as she seized the magazine and spread it out on the table in front of her. Hunky men were looking for brides? Was this for real?

Sure enough, the picture above the headline showed a small town, tucked into the gentle embrace of thick, lush forests and reaching, breathtaking mountains. Another picture, inset into the article, showed a long-angled shot of a cute old-fashioned town and a sign that read, Welcome to Treasure Creek.

"A customer left that behind." The waitress returned, overturned the cup and poured. "Interesting article. If I was single, I might hop in the car and go take a look. I mean, good, decent single men are hard to find."

"And even when you do, they have commitment issues."

"Amen, sister." The waitress set the carafe down and hauled out her notepad. "Does anything on the menu look good?"

Maybe she could eat. She ordered a cup of soup and

a club sandwich and turned her attention back to the *Now Woman* magazine article.

"Think all the good men are taken? Not so in tiny, charming Treasure Creek, Alaska, population 724. The hunky inhabitants are churchgoing, marriage-minded single men in a town with one woman for every five men! Many of them are tour guides for the town's popular tour company, Alaska's Treasures."

Churchgoing and marriage-minded sounded good. In fact, it sounded heaven-sent. She grabbed the sugar jar and upended it over the steaming cup, stirring it into the black, tarry brew as she kept reading....

"Alaska's Treasures is run by the founder's widow, Amy James. They're the best tour guides in the state, she says, proudly. And they're the hottest, ladies. A handsome pediatrician, originally from the big city, moonlights as a tour guide along the famous Klondike Highway, the very route taken by the gold rush stampede of 1898. No worries if you break a nail on the trail, ladies, he'll be right there to mend it!"

A glossy photograph of a totally hunky man with brownish hair and blue eyes stared back at her. The caption underneath the picture stated jauntily, "Doctor Alex Havens is single, ladies!"

Not bad. Karenna took a sip of coffee, let the heat and sweetness roll over her tongue. Rain sluiced down the window, smearing the view of the outside world, making the small diner seem cozy and the agony of the morning fade a notch. If only she could make her despair fade, too.

A muffled electronic chime rang from inside her purse. She unzipped the compartment and checked her cell. Her sister calling. Karenna squeezed her eyes shut, fighting the humiliation. Her stomach knotted, knowing what Kim would say. All that money, and no wedding. All the time spent, and for nothing. Come back and try to fix things.

She took a deep breath and let it ring. She wasn't up to talking about her failures right now. What she needed was hope. She'd spent seven years of her life on a man who ran at the reality of marrying her. She'd wasted seven years loving someone who didn't truly love her back.

When she opened her eyes, the article stared up at her. She turned the page and several more hunky men smiled up at her, all proclaimed bachelors, each handsome face looking like Mr. Right. Maybe these Alaska bachelors were the kind of men who knew how to keep promises and make commitments, men of honor and great of heart. Interested, she kept reading.

"So many of the guides, from the hunky chief of police to the strapping commercial fishermen, are among Alaska's Most Eligible bachelors. So, ladies, if you're looking for the adventure vacation of a lifetime that just might last a lifetime, what are you waiting for?"

Thirty-eight hours, forty-two minutes and a few coffee breaks later...

Chapter One

"I've got more diapers and formula," Gage Parker grumbled into the pay phone on the corner of the town's main street. Treasure Creek, Alaska, sandwiched between rugged snowcapped peaks and pristine forests, was an old gold-rush town currently jam-packed with women, thanks to some magazine article. He couldn't hear a single word his grandmother said, because a pair of fancy women strolled by the booth, talking and giggling and commenting on how quaint everything was.

He didn't like "quaint" and he didn't like giggling women. Women were everywhere in a town where females were usually scarce. They'd all flown in with their mounds of luggage and driven in with their city cars—not a four-wheel-drive among them. Even in the falling twilight, he could see them. They strolled the sidewalks, took up tables at Lizbet's Diner and went exploring in the wilderness, which is why he was out at nine forty-five at night when any sensible person would be home. But no, some clueless woman had gotten herself stuck halfway up a cliff this evening and he'd been on the search-and-rescue team that rapelled down to save her.

"I didn't know rock climbing would be so hard," the clueless gal had breathlessly explained, once she was clipped in and safely against his chest. She smiled coyly up at him. "My, don't you have strong arms."

Ugh. The lack of needy women was one of the big draws for moving from Seattle back to Alaska. His grandmother needing help had been the other.

"Sounds like all kinds of commotion is going on," Gran chirped, downright chipper on the other end of the line. She would be. Nothing tickled her more than that article telling about how Treasure Creek's men wanting for wives seriously outnumbered the available women. "Any of those gals catch your fancy, Gage?"

"Wishful thinking on your part. There would have to be something wrong with a woman to want to get tangled up with the likes of me." He had proof of that in his ex-wife, who had been one of those women who'd wanted a wedding but not marriage. She'd seen her vows as merely a suggestion on how to behave as a wife. "Anything else you need me to do in town?"

"I'll take pity on you, my boy, and I won't tell you to find a nice girl and bring her on home—at least this time. You already know the baby could use a mama."

Oh, she was having a heyday. Gage shook his head, trying to drum up some patience. He didn't want to hurt the elderly woman's tender feelings. "My nephew is doing just fine with the two of us. What I need is to find the right nanny, not a wife—just so we're clear on that."

"That won't stop me from praying the right woman for you comes along."

Great. More prayers. Just what he needed. God had

better things to do than trying to fix the impossible. The darkness he'd seen in his recent life had only reinforced that. His baby nephew's mother had died, his brother had been too busy to raise the child and dumped him off just shy of a week ago. Ben James, Gage's boss and one of his close friends, had died in an on-the-job accident in January, leaving his wife, Amy, a widow, with two young sons and a struggling business. Not to mention his own fight to recover from a bitter divorce. That was plenty enough disillusion to go around.

Yep, there didn't seem much reason to believe God was up there looking out for him. Not these days. He shook his head. "Gran, I'm going to pretend you didn't say that and head home."

"You and that surly disposition of yours. You had better shape up. You never know when your future wife will come along and you go and scare her off. Why, you could meet her on the street tonight."

"Sure, she *could* fall from the sky like manna from heaven." He did his best not too sound too cynical. His grandmother was a firm believer. He didn't want to mar that for her. He wished he had her strength of faith—a strength she maintained despite all her life's hardships.

He ended the call and grumbled because his cell phone had run out of juice. He wove around another pair of women dressed up in what they thought was Alaska garb, who probably had bought their pricey outfits in some fancy boutique in Beverly Hills. Ridiculous. Thoroughly disgruntled, he hopped into his four-wheel-drive. He pulled his black SUV away from the curb and had to wait for someone in a Porsche—what were people thinking?—to squeeze into a space between a tractor and an ancient pickup, before he could motor away from the madness.

On the outskirts of town, he breathed a pent-up sigh of relief. He hadn't dealt with traffic congestion since he'd been commuting across Seattle's Evergreen Bridge twice a day.

His hands were white-knuckled on the steering wheel, a bead of sweat trickled down the back of his neck. By the time he'd turned off the main road from town and headed home, twilight was deepening. He switched the vehicle's headlights to bright. The beams swept the shadowed, narrow two-lane road, illuminating undergrowth, a long wood fence line and two grazing deer, who fled into the woods.

Something reflected up ahead. He slowed down, a bad feeling settling into his gut. It looked like dark taillights and the back window of a sports car. Not a car he recognized, and he knew everyone who lived on this road. Not one of his neighbors would be foolish enough to own a car they couldn't drive when the weather turned and the roads muddied up.

Probably another one of those desperate women.

Great. Just what he needed. His grip on the steering wheel tightened. Tension seeped back into his muscles. He slowed down, close enough to make out a faded-purple Fiat perched on the narrow shoulder. The hood was up and the car appeared abandoned. A torn sign hung from the back window, bearing a single, bright pink word: *Just.*

He rolled to a stop and something white moved from behind the raised hood and into the sweep of his high beams. A woman. No, a bride. He dimmed the lights and hopped out of his rig. He noticed the Washington state plates, an expired UW parking permit decal in the window and the bad feeling in his gut turned into an ulcer. Not just another one of those marriage-crazy women who'd come to town, but this one had brought her wedding dress. How enterprising. Looked like she was having a bit of trouble, and not just with the car. He wondered what happened to the "Married" part of the sign, a sign that looked as tattered as she did.

"What are you doing here? This is a private road," he bellowed.

"Yes, I figured that out as soon as I turned onto it. But is there a place to turn around anywhere? No." She marched toward him, apparently not at all a shy, retiring sort of woman. He placed her as somewhere in her early to midtwenties. Fury punctuated every word and pounded in her heeled footsteps. "Obviously, I'm having car trouble. Do I look like I want to be here?"

"It's hard to say, with the dress."

"Oh, don't even mention that." Her eyes flared.

She could be a cute little thing if she wasn't so angry. Note to self: *Don't let this one too close.* It wasn't often a man got to see what lurked beneath a woman's guileless face and pretty smile before they said "I do." What he could already see was a major turn-off. He took a step back, because he didn't need this kind of a headache. He had enough of his own. "I'll put a call in and get a tow truck out here."

"Great. You have a cell phone?"

"Not a working one."

"You don't? You're kidding, right? Mine wouldn't get reception out here. Stupid phone." She hiked up her skirt and gave the Fiat's back tire a hard kick. "Stupid car."

"Ordinarily, I'd worry about a woman alone at night, but my guess is that you can hold your own against any threat, including a bear." No doubt a grizzly would take a look at her and run.

"Bears?" The anger drained away. She turned to face him, standing full in the light. Soft golden curls tumbled to her shoulders and framed a face that was both beautiful and unique. Big china-blue eyes dominated her pixie face, with a perfect slope of a nose and a mouth that had to have been sculpted by angels. "Are there really bears here?"

"Yes, but not many would want to take you on." Maybe he'd better look at her engine first, then figure out what to do with her. "What's with the car?"

"It started smoking. The temperature thingy has been higher than normal for a while. I think from about Vancouver on."

"British Columbia?" He grabbed the flashlight he kept behind the seat.

"But a few miles down the road it started creeping into the red zone. There was no place to stop, so I turned in here, thinking there might be a house. But there are only trees."

"And your husband? Didn't he have the sense to check the fluids?" *Please tell me there is a husband,* he thought. "Where is he?"

"No idea."

Figures. Love and marriage were supposed to *mean* something, but not to this flighty woman. "Why did you leave him? What was the problem? He wouldn't do what you wanted? Wouldn't take you on the honeymoon of your dreams? Give you every little thing you demanded?"

"Not your business." The anger returned, her soft jawline went rigid and her hands turned into fists that looked ready to punch something. Maybe him. "What about the tow truck?"

"I'm going to have to call from home, but I'm not wild about taking you to my house."

"Me, either." She hiked up her chin. "Where's the closest residence? I was about to grab my things and start walking, but I didn't know which way to go. I haven't seen anyone so far on this road."

"Myron lives up a ways. You're right. It's too far to walk. I'll take you there. Get in." He didn't sound happy about it.

That made two of them. She yanked open the Fiat's door and pain shot through her fingertip. Another broken nail. The third one to break on this impulsive trip. So much for her pre-wedding spa day. What had she been thinking?

She hadn't been. She'd been driving on pure anger, coffee and heartbreak all the way. She yanked her purse off the seat and followed the mountain man to his SUV. Maybe she should introduce herself. "I'm Karenna Digby."

"Gage Parker." He wasn't a friendly sort, and there was no missing the frown he tossed at her. No doubt he didn't think much of her.

And why would he? She looked a fright. If only she wasn't wearing this stupid gown. This dress had been the start of her problems—the catalyst that set everything in motion. The gown she *had* to have, that had cost three months of her salary, because it had represented everything she'd prayed for as a little girl.

She gathered up her train, climbed into the passenger seat and groaned at the pristine condition of the leather. She sat down, wincing because she wasn't exactly sure how much dirt, mud and grease was on her skirt. Should she apologize ahead of time? One sideways glance at Gage Parker made her change her mind about saying anything at all. Stoic guy, dark look, scary frown. Best to clean up any grime she left behind after she'd gotten out of the vehicle.

He slammed her door, circled in front of his Jeep and stalked through the headlights like a Sasquatch. He was deep shadows, big brawn and leashed power. Suddenly the shadowy woods seemed enormous and she felt very small. Miniscule, in fact. She'd been so steamed about Alan leaving her at the church, her broken-down car and her emotional decision to drive all the way to Alaska, it hadn't even occurred to her she was alone with a strange man. Sitting in his SUV. He could be a rapist or a serial killer who lived in a weird cabin, miles from known civilization.

The driver's door swung open and he angled in behind the wheel. No smile, no reassuring clue to signify he was a decent, respectable, law-abiding, nondangerous man. The dome light winked out, leaving him in shadow, making it easier to think the worst.

Okay, I'm out of my element, alone in the dark. Could You please send me a little sign here, Lord? Just something, so I know I'm all right? She knew the Lord might be busy. There was a world of strife and suffering He was tending to, but she still hoped for a small heavenly hint before the SUV started to roll and it was too late to jump out.

"When you get to Myron's, be sure you call the hotel so they can hold your room." The mountain man eased his vehicle around her disabled car and accelerated along the road. Twilit forests and a pair of antlers on a startled-looking deer sped past her window.

"My room?" She bit her lip, not quite wanting to

admit the truth to the imposing man. Of course he would
assume she had a reservation. Any sensible person
would. But had she taken the time? No. She'd been
too wound up and upset over Alan's hastily scrawled
note.

"I don't love you enough to marry you," he'd written.
"You're just too much to deal with."

"You have a room, right?" Mr. Imposing glowered at
her. The look on his face clearly said he thought she was
one of those stupid women who wouldn't have planned
ahead.

Since she'd used that word a lot over the last thirty-
eight and a half hours, she couldn't argue with him. Her
mother's voice blasted in her head like a badly burned
CD. "You have no common sense, Karenna. You don't
think things through. Who can blame Alan for chicken-
ing out? I don't know if I can ever forgive you."

No place to sleep. Another inadvertent blunder. She
should have done an Internet search for Treasure Creek
hotels. Now what? She couldn't look at Mr. Disapproving, so she pulled at a loose thread on her embroidered
skirt. "This wasn't exactly a planned trip. I figured I
could find something once I was here."

"Do you realize half the women in the contiguous
United States are in Treasure Creek? At least it seems
that way. There can't be an available hotel room within
fifty miles."

She hadn't been the only one to read the article.
Of course. She hadn't looked before she leaped. She'd
been too busy trying to escape her grief. How could she
admit that out loud? She would have to talk about what
happened—about her shattered hopes and Alan's hurtful
letter. Better to let this guy think she was a flake in a
ruined wedding dress.

She twisted in the seat to take one last look at the shadowed hump of her car on the lonely road. That's when she noticed something in the man's backseat. A baby's car seat. Tension rushed out of her and Gage Parker no longer looked intimidating or questionable. Strong and stoic and grim, maybe, but he was a father. A decent family man. That meant his wife and child were waiting for him at home. No wonder he was put out.

"Without a reservation, you're probably out of luck," he growled, wheeling his vehicle off the road and down a bumpy dirt driveway. "Myron might be able to suggest someone who could put you up for the night."

"You mean stay in someone's house?"

"Don't figure there's any room at the boarding house, either. Which means there are no other options, unless you want to sleep in your car. Maybe you want to try to find that husband of yours? He might have dug up a room somewhere."

"I wouldn't want to do that, since I didn't exactly marry him."

"Why am I not surprised?" His scowl deepened, emphasizing the crinkles in the corners of his eyes, age lines that placed him somewhere in his midthirties.

Maybe he was feeling sympathy for Alan. Maybe Gage Parker would agree with her mother's assessment of things. Karenna hung her head, not knowing what else to say.

She didn't so much care what the mountain man thought of her. She was starting to see his point. This is what happened when you acted out of upset, not calm, rational thought. She had no idea when calm, rational thought was going to kick in. She prayed it would be any second.

A glaze of lights glowed in the shadows up ahead. It was hard to see the surrounding area because of the dense trees, but she caught an impression of a big shed, a woodpile stacked higher than a house and a ramshackle cabin with torn curtains in the windows. The door swung open and a gnarled man's silhouette was backlit by the light as he put a round into the chamber of the biggest rifle Karenna had ever seen.

"Ho there," Gage called through the open window, as he stopped the Jeep. "Myron, I need to use your phone."

"Is that you, Parker?" The man ambled onto a broken-down porch and squinted at the windshield. "Is that the gal you rescued from the cliff?"

"Nah. This is a different one. Her car died out on the road." He opened the door and hopped to the ground. An old hound dog loped around the side of the house, yowling. Gage paid it no heed. "She needs a tow truck. You wouldn't mind if she waited with you, right?"

"What? Are you kiddin'?" The old man moved down a few steps and glared harder at her. She could feel his disapproval piercing the tempered glass. "Is that a weddin' dress she's wearin'? I don't want nothin' to do with that."

"C'mon, Myron. You know I've got my hands full at home." Gage's voice was a murmur now, as the two men bent together conspiratorially in the poorly lit front yard. The hound put his paws on the edge of the driver's seat, sniffed the air and barked at her. No way was she able to hear what was going on.

What she needed was to get out of the vehicle and beg the old man to help her. Although it did look kind of scary out there, so shadowy, with the forest right up next to the buildings. Surely, he was a kind soul who wouldn't turn away a woman in need? Hadn't the magazine article said the town was full of noble men and handsome hero types? She opened her door and something big, furry and black lunged at her.

Yikes. A bear! She pulled the door closed with all her might and screamed when something hit the window. Beady green eyes glowed through the glass. Fear exploded through her and she flew out of the seat. The belt yanked tight, holding her in place.

The dog silenced, Gage hopped behind the wheel and slammed the door. "That's a no go. I can't believe Myron. He doesn't like brides, either."

"B-bear," she sputtered out, pointing at the window. The beast beat against the glass again, rocking the Jeep.

"That's Myron's other dog." Gage shook his head at her. "You don't know much, do you?"

That's exactly what Alan used to say to her. The big black creature loped through the gray twilight—now clearly a mammoth dog—as he joined the grizzled old man on the porch.

She might not know much, but she was learning. Life used to be simple, but it had gone from great to complicated in five seconds flat, and she hadn't been prepared. Add that to the fact that she was out of her element and she hadn't slept in nearly two days—and she was a mess. "What now? Are you going to take me back to my car for the night?"

"No." He sounded unhappy as he wheeled his vehicle around and pointed the headlights down the sorry excuse for a driveway. "You're coming home with me. But there are going to be rules."

"Yes, absolutely." She thought of the wife and child at home, missing him, maybe wondering why he was late. Some women might not be understanding of a husband arriving with a younger woman in tow. "I really appreciate this, Mr. Parker."

"You're not to disrupt things. I've got a baby in the house. Matthew needs to stay on his schedule."

"Of course." Matthew. A little boy. "How old is your son?"

"He's my nephew. Apparently, my brother decided he had better things to do than raise him, so I'm doing it by default."

"You and your wife must be extraordinary people, to take in a baby."

"My wife? That's a good one." He shook his head, the SUV accelerating on the dirt lane. They bounced harder until he hit the brakes with an angry punch. The seat belt caught her again, saving her from hitting the dash. "No wife. She had better things to do than stay married to me."

"I'm sorry." She could tell the man was hurting. She could make a huge list of all the obvious differences between them, but they had the ravages of failed relationships in common. She felt sorry for him. "I wish that hadn't happened to you."

He glanced at her sideways as he turned off the narrow country road. Surprise carved into his granite features. He really was a handsome man. Dark, thick hair tumbled over a high forehead. His compelling sky-blue eyes and high slash of cheekbones could have belonged to a movie star. The straight blade of his nose didn't overpower his face, and his mouth and jaw were pure artistry.

If only he didn't scowl so much.

"Don't get any ideas," he said. "I'm off the market for good."

"Ideas?" She blinked. "You mean marriage?"

"Yes." He didn't sound as if he thought she was too bright, either. "That's another rule. If you want me to help you, you don't try any funny stuff."

"Funny stuff?"

"Flirting. And don't even try to get on my grand-mother's good side." He sounded angrier and angrier.

She wasn't exactly impressed. In fact, she was liking him less and less with every passing second. "You live with your grandmother?"

"Remember what I said." He maneuvered along a tree-lined driveway and gravel crunched beneath the tires. "You leave with the tow truck. Got it?"

"Like I would want to stay." It wasn't such a mystery why he was divorced. His plan was sounding like a really good idea. She didn't want to spend any more time with Mr. Bitter than necessary. She didn't want his mood or his personality to rub off on her.

Chapter Two

Gage watched the front door of the two-story log home open in a wash of light. Like a beacon, it drew him and Miss Digby closer. A diminutive woman's shadow appeared in the doorway, drawing a sweater over her shoulders against the cooling night air. No doubt Gran had caught sight of Miss Digby in the Jeep when he'd pulled up, and she was busy drawing all kinds of wrong conclusions.

So not looking forward to this, he thought, and stepped aside to let the jilted bride go first. Karenna swished ahead of him up the concrete walkway and into the porch light's reach.

"Goodness! Who do we have here?" Gran practically sang, she sounded so happy. "A wayward traveler you found on the drive home?"

He groaned, bracing himself for the obvious comment yet to come—that his grandmother had prayed for him to find a woman. He was no way interested in the too-young, too-cute, too-emotional Miss Digby. He'd rather hike the entire Chilkoot Trail in his bare feet, from start to finish, than let himself be even the smallest bit interested in the woman. It didn't take a genius to know why she'd come to town. If one groom didn't work, then go grab another, right?

He frowned at his grandmother so she knew he wasn't thrilled by the situation. "She needs to use the phone."

"Yes, I got lost and then my car died," the wayward bride explained, as she gathered her skirts and hiked up the steps. Her ragged train swept along behind her. "I'm so sorry to inconvenience you."

"It's not a lick of trouble, don't you worry." Gran looked pleased as punch as she led the way into the house. "We can get Bucky to take a look at your car. Don't tell me you were on your way to your wedding?"

"More like running away from the disaster my wedding had become."

"A runaway bride. How mysterious. Come in, dear. You look as if you could use a hot cup of tea and a plate of my homemade cookies."

Never should have brought the bride home. Gage kicked his boots off on the porch and slapped himself on the forehead. Too late now. Gran looked as cozy as could be, fussing over the young woman. That was his grandmother. Nurturing to all. She looked bursting with excitement, ecstatic that her prayer had been answered. He'd found not just a woman on the way home, but one in a wedding gown.

He stormed into the foyer with shopping bags in hand, and gave the door a shove. The resulting bang reverberated through the house, surprising even him.

"Gage." Gran looked up from the archway into the kitchen. She winced when a baby's crying erupted upstairs. "Look what you've done. You've woken Matthew."

"Sorry." He shrugged out of his coat, mad at himself and wishing he could have a do-over on his day. "Want me to get him?"

"You? What do you know about babies?" Gran shook her head, as if she were sorry he'd turned out the way he had. He didn't know a thing about infants, it was true. She said something to Karenna before disappearing up the stairwell.

He hung his jacket on a wall hook and realized he was alone in the living room. Where had the Digby woman gone? She'd been here a second ago. He followed the sound of water running to the kitchen. She stood at the sink filling the tea kettle.

Interesting.

He set the shopping bag on the counter. "Making yourself at home?"

"I thought I would help out. I don't feel right, having your grandmother wait on me." She spun the few steps to the stove and flipped on a burner.

"Then feel free to help yourself to the phone." He nodded toward the wall phone hanging near the refrigerator. "The local yellow pages are in the top drawer. There are two listings for tow trucks, but Bucky is the one still in business."

"Why don't you like me?" She hitched her chin up a notch, studying him with blue eyes capable of bending unsuspecting men to her will.

"What's not to like?" He grabbed a bottle of root beer from the fridge and twisted the cap. "As far as I can tell, you ran out on your wedding. What you're doing here in a wedding dress is anyone's guess. Why didn't you change on the way? Or did you think the men here would be rubes, easily tricked into marrying you—so you didn't bother to change?"

"Believe me, if you are anything like the rest of the men in this town, then I want to sue that magazine for false reporting. You are hardly hunky, marriage-minded or charming." Okay, maybe she'd gotten carried away. Gage Parker *was* hunky, but that was about all the good she could say about him.

The baby's crying grew louder as he grew closer, and she gave the disagreeable mountain man a wide berth as she eased by. Disdain rolled off him in waves.

It didn't take a genius to guess his story. He'd been so disagreeable, his wife had left him, which had only embittered him more. Sympathy filled her. She knew firsthand how painful that cycle could be. She was a child of divorce. Her parents had battled each other until their bond and their marriage had been nothing but dust and broken promises.

With the way Alan had bailed on her, she could understand the allure of bitterness and blame. She was struggling not to give in to the darker side of her anger. Seeing Gage Parker's life, living with his grandmother because he'd chased everyone else away, was a good reminder to her. Get the anger out, let go and let God lead her to a better place.

She'd pray for Gage, she decided, glancing over her shoulder. He had made a beeline to the phone and began dialing. No guess as to who he was calling. He did *not* look happy with her.

"Shhh, little Matthew," Gage's grandmother said soothing the baby's cries in the homey living room. She cradled a blue-wrapped bundle cozily between her neck and her shoulder, one fragile hand caressing small circles against the baby's back. "It's all right now. There will be no more scary noises, I can promise you that."

Karenna caught a glimpse of the baby's red face and her heart broke at his misery. Poor little guy. She took one look at the older woman, her features hollow with exhaustion. Dark shadows bruised the skin beneath her eyes. Was she the infant's sole caretaker? That was a worthy job, but a very demanding one, especially for this frail woman who looked to be struggling with the workload. What was Gage thinking? Determined to help, Karenna bounded through the living room, her own upset and tiredness forgotten.

"Someone's having a rough night." She tried to get a better look at the baby. He had a shock of dark hair, and big animated eyes and the cutest button face, scrunched up and tear stained. She placed him around six months old. His hands waved, fisted, with the strength of his sobs. She reached out for the little guy. "Let me take him for you."

"So you know about babies?" The woman handed over the tyke with smiling approval.

"I worked in a day-care center. A very good one, I'm proud to say, ma'am." She settled Matthew into the curve of her arm, hurting right along with him. "It's hard being little, isn't it? You sound hungry to me. Is that a hungry cry?"

"You can call me Jean, dear. I'll warm a bottle." Jean jumped toward the kitchen, eager to help. Easy to see the endless love she had for her great-grandchild.

"I can do it while I'm waiting for the tow truck. After all, you've had the day shift. You must be tired." She gently rocked the child in her arms. "Sit down and relax."

"What a dear you are, Karenna." Jean beamed with gratitude. "It *has* been a wearying day."

"Then put your feet up. I've got this covered." She shared a smile with the elderly woman before retracing her steps to the kitchen. She began to hum the first tune that popped into her head, "Jesus Loves Me." Matthew's crying toned down a notch and his dark blue eyes searched hers. One tiny hiccup and he silenced, gazing up at her intently.

"There now, see? Everything is fine." She hardly noticed the big surly man standing like a hulk in the center of the kitchen. Easy enough to skirt on by him. She tugged open the fridge. "We'll get your bottle warm and food in your tummy. Wouldn't that feel wonderful?"

"This isn't going to work, you know." Gage's frown blasted her like icy wind off a glacier.

"Why? Is there something wrong with the stove?" She transferred a bottle from the refrigerator shelf onto the countertop.

"I'm not talking about the formula. You're trying to win over my grandmother. I told you I wasn't going to put up with any manipulation like that."

"Manipulation?" Confused, she opened a lower cabinet and spied a pan. She snatched it by the handle and stepped around the glowering man. Again. "Sorry. You're wrong about that. I only want to help."

"But why?" He took the pan from her and turned on the tap. Water rushed in, and he studied her through his lashes, trying to figure out her angle.

"Because it's a lot of work to take good care of an infant, something Jean is obviously trying very hard to do. Anyone can see she needs a hand. It's a lot to juggle all by herself, especially when the baby is down for the night and some man thoughtlessly wakes him up."

"Okay, I shouldn't have let the door slam. My fault." The pan was full, so he walked it over to the stove. "It's decent of you to lend a hand."

"Especially since you didn't seem inclined to do it." She plunked the bottle into the water and spun the dial. She smelled like roses and springtime, and this close, beneath the bright fluorescent lights, he noticed a tiny blanket of freckles across her nose and the unmistakable signs of exhaustion on her face.

"I don't know much about babies. That's why I can't help." He turned away, furious at himself. He had no business looking at her long enough to notice anything. She was too young, too pretty, too infuriating and she didn't belong here.

"You can learn—*then* you could help." Her tone had softened. That couldn't be compassion he heard in her voice, a warm understanding that reached out to him like a balm to his wounds.

He didn't need it. He didn't need anyone or anything. "I know. Gran can't keep doing this all alone. She has health concerns."

"I wondered." Gentle, her voice low now, so it wouldn't carry into the living room. "Look at him. He's blowing bubbles. You're a good boy, Matthew. Yes, you are."

He watched Karenna change before his eyes. Her voice became song and her face took on immeasurable beauty. Loving goodness emanated from her as she gently rocked the baby in her arms. Every fiber of her being seemed focused on Matthew. Amazing. He could be fooled into thinking she was the answer to one of his biggest problems.

The phone rang, drowning out the first notes as her humming turned to singing. He recognized the chorus of "Jesus Loves Me" as he grabbed the receiver. Please let it be Bucky on his way with the tow truck. "Hello?"

"Gage." Bucky's easygoing drawl reeled across the line. What a relief. "Got your message. Sorry I won't be able to make it out your way until tomorrow. I've got four other calls lined up before yours, and no way can I work through the night."

"Four other calls?" He couldn't have heard right. No, this had to be a bad dream. A nightmare. Maybe he'd only *dreamed* he'd woken up this morning, went to work taking a raft of city women downriver, answered the search-and-rescue call. If none of it was real, then he would be wake up and Karenna would be gone from his kitchen and his life.

If only.

"It's all these marriage-minded women. Woo-ee," Bucky was saying. "It's a gold rush of a different kind—romance. They say love's the greatest treasure. I ain't had this kind of attention since, well, never. I'll be there when I can, Gage."

"Bucky. Don't hang up—" Too late. The call disconnected and dial tone buzzed in his ear. Great. Just what he needed. Maybe he could take a look at the car himself. Maybe it just needed a little water and it could make it to town….

Wishful thinking, and he knew it. He was doomed. Worse, he should have been more like Myron. Recognized the danger of a bride without a wedding ring and kept driving right on by her.

Too bad he wasn't that kind of man.

"Was that the tow truck guy?" She swept the rumbling tea kettle off the stove with one hand, moving easily, keeping her attention on the baby, completely competent and in her element.

Careful, man. Don't let your opinion of her change. It was the best weapon he had to keep her at bay. He managed a nod and somehow spoke past the sudden tightness in his throat. "He won't be able to come until tomorrow morning. I'll see if I can't find you a place to stay for the night."

"That would be decent of you." She smiled shyly at him—not flirty, not coy, not manipulative. Worry shadowed her, but she looked as if she were trying to hide it.

He took the tea kettle from her and filled the three cups she'd set out, ignoring the sensation of being close to her. If his pulse kicked up a notch, it was probably from the ire of being forced to deal with her.

What did he do about tonight? Chances were slim he could find an available room, but he had to try. He grabbed the phone book, leafed through the pages and squinted at the fine print.

"I made you some chamomile tea." She slid the mug onto the counter beside him. "Looks like you could use something soothing. I didn't mean to add to your stress. You look as if you've had a rough day."

"I'm fine," he bit out, trying to find a reason—any reason—to dislike her more. She didn't seem dippy at all—or flighty or manipulative—and he wanted her to be. He wished he felt that she was taking advantage of him and trying to play with his feelings.

But no, that was another woman who had been guilty of that. His wife had done a number on him, no doubt about it. He hated to admit he was wrong. Karenna Digby didn't seem a threat as she moved away with the cup of tea for his grandmother, and left the room with it.

He could hear the lullaby of her voice as she exchanged words with Gran in the living room. He punched in the phone number and waited for it to connect. No room at the inn, he was told, so he punched in the next number. There were only a few hotels in town, plus the boarding house. By the time Karenna had returned to whisk the bottle from the boiling water and test the formula on her wrist, he'd made his last call. Looked like he was stuck with her.

"What a good boy," Karenna whispered at the crib rail, latching it securely. One look at Matthew asleep in his fluffy blue sleeper made her melt. Such a little doll. She had a soft spot for all babies. It's what had made her good at her job and what she hoped would make her a good mom one day.

That day was now a lot farther in the future.

She took one last look at the sleeping baby, asked God and His angels to watch over the child and padded into the hallway. She drew the door closed behind her, hoping Gage had found her a place for the night. If not, she always had her car.

"Thanks for helping out." Gage was sitting in the mostly dark living room. He'd turned all but one lamp off, and he rose, merging with the shadows. "Taking care of the baby is too much for Gran to do alone day in and day out."

"Isn't there anyone else to help?"

"No family close by, and I haven't found a nanny. Don't think I haven't tried. Until a few days ago there was a serious scarcity of women in these parts."

"So I read." It had seemed eons ago when she'd spotted the little diner north of Bellingham and stopped for coffee. The jury was still out on whether her decision to drive to Alaska had been a good one, but she was hopeful. "Since the hotels are brimming with women, I'm sure you can find someone to hire who won't mind your surly disposition."

"Or maybe they are too desperate for marriage to care about my disposition." A hint of humor warmed his words.

"I suppose that's what you think I am. Desperate. An opportunist looking for a man." She spotted her purse on the vanity table behind the sofa and circled around to fetch it. "You think that I heard there were available bachelors and I couldn't get here fast enough to catch one of them."

"That's how it looks." He moved toward her to stop her from grabbing her purse. "Someone only out for herself and her own gain wouldn't have waited on Gran, taken care of Matthew, put both of them to bed and then cleaned up the kitchen. And all done with a smile on your face."

"I like to help people." She figured there was a lot more she could tell him. How she'd disappointed her upwardly mobile parents, who were a tad on the ruthless side, by choosing to take care of babies instead of pursuing a white-collar profession, which they thought was the only acceptable pathway. How her mother had told her after reading Alan's letter, "I'm so ashamed of you, Karenna."

No, best to keep those things to herself. "I figured I owed you, seeing as how you could have left me with Myron and his bear, even if I wasn't welcome."

"That dog *does* look like a bear—and acts like one, too. I couldn't do that, even to you." Was that a smile in his voice?

Maybe just a little one, she decided, realizing she

was smiling, too. "I hate to impose, but could I borrow a blanket and a pillow?"

"What for?"

"To make my front seat a little more comfortable. I *had* to buy the fun car instead of being sensible and getting a sedan with a backseat." She rolled her eyes. "What was I thinking?"

"That you wouldn't be stuck on a country road in Alaska overnight?"

"Right. I'm mostly a stay-close-to-home kind of girl. What I'm doing here, I have no real idea. Especially since I just figured out you can't run from what's hurting you."

"It comes right along with you. Yep, I learned that the hard way, too." He felt unusually close as he cleared his throat. "About the car. I think it's a bad idea."

"Because of bears?"

"Because it's not right. I changed the sheets on the bed upstairs while you were in the kitchen. There's fresh towels in the bathroom and a few of Gran's things folded on the dresser. Have a good night."

"But where will you sleep?"

"The couch will suit me fine." He brushed passed her and reached for the remote. He flipped on the late-night news and hunkered down in a recliner to watch.

"Thank you, Gage." She thought she felt him smile again as she padded up the stairs, but the mountain man was still too much of a mystery for her to be sure.

Chapter Three

Karenna in the morning was a sight to behold. Gage nearly dropped the coffee pot when she strolled into the kitchen. Good thing the thermos was nearly full. He set the carafe back on the burner with an unsteady hand. Strange that he would react to her like that. He gave a single nod of recognition as she opened a cabinet and helped herself to a coffee cup.

"Good morning." She appeared as if she meant it, for her too-big and impossibly blue eyes were sparkling. She looked as cute as could be, even with her golden hair damp from a shower, and she was wearing a pair of his old gray sweats. She looked like one of those cheerful morning people. "I hope you slept well? I kept worrying that you weren't comfortable on the couch."

"I noticed you were up several times during the night when Matthew cried."

"I took his crib monitor from Jean's room when she wasn't looking. I figured she could use a full night's sleep." She sidled next to him at the counter and whisked the coffeepot off the burner. "Playing nanny for a bit was the least I could do in exchange for your hospitality."

"That's decent of you." He twisted the cap on his thermos tight.

"Back at you." She poured a cup of coffee. "You look as if you're about to head out the door. Where do you work?"

"I'm a guide for a local tour company."

"The one in the magazine?"

"Yes, and don't give me that look."

"What look?" She pulled the carton of milk out of the fridge and stirred a thin stream into her coffee.

"The one that promises all of Alaska's Treasures tour guides are handsome, eligible bachelors. Obviously, they didn't include me in the article."

"Obviously."

Sure, she was beautiful. She was cute and captivating, wholesome and charming. Now that she wasn't in a wedding gown, he didn't feel nearly as defensive around her. But that didn't mean he intended to like her.

"If they had, then women like you wouldn't be flocking into town—"

"Excuse me. Women like me?" She arched a brow at him. The look on her face said, no longer wholesome. She'd morphed into the tire kicker, the woman who'd been all steamed up when he'd first come across her, stranded in the dark. She arrowed the full force of her gaze at him. "What exactly does that mean?"

"Flighty women. Women looking for advantage and opportunity."

"Oh, so now we're back to me being an opportunist. Tell me, what opportunity am I looking for? What advantage?"

"Hard to say when you're in a mood like that." Uh-oh. He'd never had a way with the ladies, and this was a flash of what had gone wrong in his marriage.

He would open his mouth very clear on his opinion of things, only to be outright misunderstood. Women. Not just a mystery to him, but to the entire universe. "Let's just say you're not the staying type."

"Staying type? Oh, and men are?" She shut the refrigerator door and stalked across the floor to glare up at him. "I just got left at the altar. Hell*o?* I wasn't the one who ran off."

"I didn't know that." This wasn't going at all the way he wanted. Panic set in, along with the fervent wish he'd gotten out the door *before* she'd come into the kitchen. "When I got divorced, I never figured I would have another irate woman to deal with before breakfast."

"Guess again, buddy." She shook her head, scattering bouncy golden locks. "I can't think of anyone who has ever gotten me so mad so fast. You have a gift, Gage."

"I've got something." A disaster record when it came to women. Good thing he was under no illusions that he ought to try marriage again. He and women just didn't mix. Like oil and water. Like gasoline and flame. Like dynamite and a detonator. "I've got to get to work. Bucky ought to be here around ten. It was real nice meeting you."

"You don't sound as if you mean that."

"I don't. Good luck, Karenna." *That* he meant.

He couldn't help the tug in his chest as he grabbed his lunch pail, his egg sandwich from the counter and his thermos. He opened the back door—didn't know why he took one last look at her.

Maybe he sort of liked her. She was spunky and perky and had been kind to Gran and Matthew. She looked out of place in the simple country kitchen, so beautiful she hurt his eyes.

He shut the door behind him, closing down his

emotions. He had no business feeling anything for her. He strode down the porch and into the morning light.

What a cantankerous man. Karenna watched Gage's SUV trail down the driveway, the taillights growing fainter until the thick stands of cedar and fir stole him from her sight. He was too young to be truly called cantankerous—that brought to mind someone at the end of his life, embittered and thoroughly disagreeable. It's more like Gage had a grizzled personality.

That, and he didn't think much of women. After putting cold water and fresh grounds into the coffeemaker, she carried her cup to the round table in the sunny breakfast nook. She was a Seattle girl, raised in the Green Lake neighborhood north of the University district, where leafy trees lined pleasant streets and a short walk took her to the small city park and lake. *That* was her idea of nature.

Not anymore. The view outside the picture window was awe-inspiring. A lush green forest marched up the hillside as far as she could see, to the lower skirt of a mountain range. Snowcapped peaks, rugged and majestic, speared the flawless blue sky, as if the earth were trying to reach all the way to heaven. What a beautiful start to a day, gazing upon all of this. Surely, living here would make someone less cantankerous over time?

A deer and two small, spotted fawns wandered into the driveway. Such tiny, delicate creatures, peaceful and sweet. She held her breath, not daring to move as they passed by the window.

"Probably come to try to nibble at my garden." Jean broke the silence, padding into the kitchen in her pink terry-cloth robe and scuffed yellow slippers. "Gage got it fenced up good and tight for me, but there's no telling if the deer will stay out. They're real inventive. Good morning, dear."

"Good morning. Did you sleep well?"

"Like a rock."

"Matthew had a bottle around four. He was sound asleep the last I checked."

"He is. I just peeked in at him. Sleeping like an angel." Jean shuffled to the coffeemaker. "I see you made fresh. Gage takes half of the pot in his work thermos."

"I wanted to make sure there was enough for you." Karenna pushed out of her chair. "I was thinking about breakfast. Would you like me to cook? I wouldn't mind."

"Oh, I couldn't let you do that. You're our guest."

"Guest? More like an imposition."

"It depends on who you are talking to." Jean appeared amused as she stirred milk into her cup. "You saw Gage before he left?"

"Saw him, talked to him, lived to regret it."

"You and everyone else." Jean laughed easily, reminding Karenna of her own grandmother. "I'm not at all sure what I'm going to do about that boy."

Boy? He was a man in his prime, wide of shoulder, brawny and strong. Karenna couldn't imagine Gage as a boy. "Was he always that impossible?"

"You mean stubborn? Strong-willed?" Jean nodded. "Yes. He was the funniest kid. Kept me in stitches the whole time he was growing up."

"Gage funny?" She fished a frying pan out of the lower cabinets. "You have to be talking about someone else. I don't buy it. Not Gage."

"He was a card. Always laughing. Always seeing the bright side of life." Jean opened the fridge and handed over a carton of eggs. "That was before his marriage fell apart. I knew that girl wasn't right for him. She was nice enough. She just didn't value all the right things, Gage especially."

"That sounds difficult." Having some experience with that very thing sent a wave of sympathy through her. Hard to picture Gage with a smile on his face, always laughing. "He must have changed completely."

"Ain't that the truth. I hardly recognize him." Jean dug through the fridge and produced a package of bacon and a pitcher of orange juice. "He's not the same man. These days, he's hard and cynical. I don't think he means to be. He's simply lost."

"Is that why he's living with you? He was recently divorced?" Karenna took the bacon and peeled off thick, smoky slices.

"No. I've been living with him for five years, going on six. This is his house. He moved back from Washington—"

"Washington *State?*" She nearly dropped the bacon on the counter.

"Some fancy Seattle suburb."

She and Gage had once lived in the same city? Scary coincidence.

"That's where Margaret *had* to live. Fancy was what mattered to her." Unlike her grandson, Jean wasn't bitter or harsh. Her lovely face crinkled with loving compassion. "I still feel so sorry for her, fighting for what could never truly make anyone happy, not in the long run. Gage was so in love with her, he wore himself out working long hours in that firm—"

"A firm?" She definitely couldn't see that. The mountain man working in a firm? Wearing a suit and tie?

"He's an architect. Leastways, that's what he went to

school for. Graduated top of his class and landed a real fine job." Pride lifted Jean up. Easy to see how much she loved her grandson. "He did real good down there. But when he came home, he wasn't the same."

"He must have truly loved her."

"He did." Jean wiped at the corner of her eyes with a napkin. "I keep praying for him. I have faith that God will lead Gage back to His heart. Our Lord won't let us down."

"He is ever-faithful." This she knew for sure. At twenty-five, she still had a lot to figure out, especially about love and life, but she *believed*. She'd felt God's touch in her life too often to doubt. Maybe He had brought her to Alaska for a reason. Maybe there was some good she could do.

"Yes, our Lord is always here with us." Jean reached out and squeezed Karenna's hand. Her touch was warm and strong, a connection between two kindred spirits. "He had a plan in bringing you to us."

"That's what I was thinking, too. I would feel much better if my emotion-fuelled drive here was for a greater purpose, and not just another big mistake of mine."

"You were led here. I know this is true. I can feel it."

"Good, because I don't want to add it to my growing pile of dumb moves." She couldn't help adoring Jean. It was as if they'd known each other for years. "And before you say it, yes, I've made a lot of major oopses. I tend to leap with both feet, *then* look."

"That's called youth." Jean stepped back to pour the orange juice. "We all have mountains of mistakes in our life. It's part of being human. Now turn the bacon, dear, before it starts to burn."

* * *

Not one of his better days. Gage rubbed at the tension headache settling deep in his right temple, opened the back door and strode into the tour office. A lot of desks were empty—most of the guides were out giving tours—but not him. No, he'd received a search-and-rescue call a second before he'd walked in the door early this morning.

A pair of hikers missing overnight, which turned out to be two women from South Beach, Florida, who'd never been in the wilderness before, didn't pack any of the necessary gear, and when he finally found them wandering the forest instead of staying in one place, each of them had a handful of wildflowers and ran toward him, diamonds and rubies and capped teeth gleaming in the sun. One woman called him her hero a second before proposing.

Of course, he'd swiftly turned her down and handed her over to another man on his team, Reed, his buddy and Treasure Creek's police chief. He noticed Reed had turned down the woman's overeager proposal, too. Wannabe brides were everywhere.

He was too smart for them. He had found out the hard way that love was a river that plunged straight off a cliff, taking the doomed with it. He stormed over to his desk, a frown brewing. He hadn't been able to force Karenna from his mind. The image of her in his kitchen, bright as the sun, cheerful as a song, stuck with him as if it had been glued to his brainpan.

With any luck, Bucky had towed her car into town and patched up the radiator, and Karenna Digby was no longer his problem. He ignored the stack of messages the receptionist, Rachel, had placed dead center on his desk, yanked open the top drawer and dug around for

a bottle of aspirin he kept on hand. He popped two
without water and spotted his boss and good friend
at her desk, her hair curtaining her face, intent on a
phone call. Tension in her jaw and tiny lines dug into
her forehead told him it wasn't a pleasant conversation.
His boots carried him forward and he arrived deskside
without thinking about it.

"Yes, you're absolutely right, Lindy." Amy James
nodded at him, while still intent on her call. "We do
need a miracle."

Lindy. There was only one Lindy in town—the owner
of the boarding house. The Lindy who hadn't been able
to help him find a room in town for Karenna. He crossed
his arms over his chest and leaned against the edge of
Amy's desk.

"Yes, of course, my great-great-grandfather's treasure map would come in awful handy about now." Amy
folded a lock of hair behind her ear, the tension in her
jaw vanishing, replaced by a hint of humor. "Too bad
it's lost for good. Sure. I'll do the impossible and loan it
to the town so we can keep the library. No problem."

Oh. The budget crisis. He knew that Lindy was on
the town council. Economic times were tough all over,
but especially in Treasure Creek. Tourist dollars drove
their economy, and with Ben's death the tour company
had nearly closed. It was an economic hardship that
rippled outward. He knew for a fact the town was considering drastic steps, like consolidating the schools,
and if things didn't improve, they would be annexed
by the county. Now it sounded like the library was in
jeopardy, too.

"Thanks, Lindy." Amy hung up the phone.

"Trouble?" he asked.

"Something like that. Lindy was just calling to

update me on the last town meeting and to book tours for some of her boarders." Amy grinned up at him. "I just made over a dozen bookings. Guess what? All of them are women."

"New to town?" he hazarded a guess.

"Exactly. Word is, they all want to meet handsome guides. They are specifically requesting the rive raft rides they read about in the magazine." Her eyes twinkled.

"This is all your fault. I'm blaming you. It's because of you all these women are here."

"It's good for our town, I have to admit, but things didn't turn out like I expected."

"Then again, what does?"

"Exactly. You know I wrote a letter to an outdoor magazine, hoping to drum up interest in our tour business. I couldn't stand to see this business my Ben built fail. The town needed the jobs. This company is the major employer in the area. I was only trying to help."

He understood. It destroyed him, too, to see the town failing and the people he'd known all of his life struggling. Amy was even more attached to this place because her great-great-grandfather, Mack Tanner, had founded the historic gold rush town and played an integral part in its success. Word was, Tanner had buried a fortune along the Chilkoot Trail, but no one had ever found it.

He'd read the original letter, so he knew exactly how well-intentioned her letter had been. The proposals and offers of help she'd received after Ben's loss touched her deeply, and she'd written about the fine men who had tried to take care of her. She could have tried to promote her company, but it had been her employees and the men of this town she'd lauded. How that caring letter had wound up on an editor's desk at a glossy women's magazine in New York City was anyone's guess. But there was no doubt the *Now Woman* magazine article had made quite a splash. The area was full of tourists—women, to be specific—who were staying in hotels, eating in local restaurants and spending money in the town shops. The good Lord surely worked in mysterious ways.

"I think we can both agree you helped. Maybe all this business will be enough to save the tour company and help with the town's deficit."

"It's hard to tell if this is a phase or a lasting thing. We can't count on it being permanent, but we can do our best to give these ladies the best tours we can." Amy pushed a schedule sheet his way. "You are booked solid for tomorrow's Gentle Waters River Rafting tour."

He glared at the list. All women. He wasn't enthused. "Yippee."

"Gage, you crack me up." Amy chuckled, shaking her head. "Why are you here anyway? I take it you found the missing hikers?"

"That's an affirmative."

"You don't seem happy. Do I dare ask what happened?"

"You *know* what happened. One of them tried to entrap me in the chains of marriage. When I sidestepped, she went after Reed."

"Reed?" The amusement slipped from Amy's face. That always happened whenever Reed's name was mentioned.

Not his business, but personally, he thought there was something between the two of them. Not that either of them knew it yet.

"Thanks for finding a sub for my morning's tour." He pushed away from her desk. "I appreciate it."

"That's the drawback of having the best search-and-rescue men on staff. I'm glad everyone was found safe."

He wasn't the best, but he didn't feel up to arguing with her. "Do you need anything done?"

"No. You may as well head home early. How are things going with the nanny hunt? You know, with all these ladies in town maybe some of them would be interested—"

"Don't even say it." The last thing he wanted to do was to entangle himself with marriage-minded women. "I'll be in bright and early tomorrow, unless I get another emergency call."

"You've been getting a lot of those lately." She was smiling again. She knew how much it tortured him.

Not that he minded rescuing women—but to have them propose? And they hadn't even bothered to read up on basic outdoor skills.

Take the women he'd found today—not a single survival skill between them two of them. The ending could have been very different. He gave thanks to the Lord all had ended well—except for the marriage proposal.

Now he only had one marriage-minded female on his mind, and he grabbed the phone at his desk to dial home. After a few reassurances from Gran that Karenna Digby was gone from both his life and his house, then he could hop into his truck and head home without fear. He was not going to be stuck with Karenna for another night. But the phone rang four times and the answering machine came on.

That isn't a sign of doom, he told himself, as he hiked out the back door. Gran might be upstairs getting

Matthew up from his nap. She might be outside weeding the garden. There was a long list of reasons why she didn't pick up and why Karenna would be gone. Not that he felt ready to risk a trip home to find out, so he bypassed his truck in the lot and circled around to the sidewalk. He'd be smart and run a few errands first.

"Yo there, Gage." Bucky looked up from behind a luxury sedan's hood and grinned like a toothpaste commercial actor. The mechanic was twenty-six, had played quarterback on the high-school football team back in the day, and had lately taken over his dad's garage. All-American, golden-haired, blue-eyed and square-jawed, he was exactly what women like Karenna had flocked to Treasure Creek to find.

Great. Gage couldn't explain why that ticked him off. Just that it did. He felt lacking. Doing his best not to show it, he managed what he hoped was a pleasant smile. "Looks like you're doing a bit of work. Did you get a chance to look at Miss Digby's car?"

"You mean Karenna? Truth is, I'm over my head, between towing and doing repairs." He straightened up and circled around the side of the car. He wiped his hands on a purple, grease-stained rag. "Truth be told, it took longer cuz I'm getting to meet some of the fine ladies come to town. Woo-hee, I've never had so much fun doin' my job before."

"So I see." At least someone was enjoying the madness. "The car?"

"Karenna sure is a pretty gal. I saw her when I went to your house this morning." Bucky lit up like the Fourth of July—sparkling eyes and beaming expectations. "Sure seems nice, too, helpin' out your gramma with the housework. And the way that baby took to her.

She'd make a real fine wife. Here's prayin' she stays in town so I get a chance with her."

Hard to say why that made him see red. "What about all the other women who seem to suddenly have car trouble? You want a chance with them, too?"

"One at a time. Got to prioritize." Bucky looked like a kid in a candy store—one that could have anything he wanted and had already made his choice.

Gage ought to be happy at getting Karenna out of his house and out of his life. So why wasn't he?

"Can you fix her car?"

"No problem. I just need to replace the radiator. I've got her Fiat in one of the bays." Bucky stuck the hand rag in his back overalls pocket. "I'll get to it right away. Wish me luck with her."

"Good luck." He didn't know what else to say as he walked on by. Couldn't explain the lingering sadness that hit him. She was gone from his life. Good. He ought to be relieved. He was glad to see her go.

The hard knot in his chest wasn't jealousy, he told himself as he glanced around town. The sidewalk was packed and he had to dodge women as he made a beeline for the general store. Bucky was perfect for Karenna. They were both as idealistic as could be, and that woman was trouble, sure as shootin'.

And to make things worse, he'd been unable to stop thinking about her most of the day. The image of Karenna in his kitchen last night, beautiful in spite of the torn and stained gown, haunted him. She made an incredible bride, but she was naïve and unrealistic. He wished he had told her more about what had happened to his marriage. Maybe she could have used a word of warning.

Now it was too late. She was gone. No reason to

see her again, and it wasn't as if he intended to look her up. He knew from firsthand experience what was going to happen to her. After she hooked herself another groom—maybe even Bucky—she would surely get hurt, and the light would dim from her beautiful spirit for good. If she didn't know about the plunging off the cliff part of marriage, then she would learn the hard way, just like he did.

Gage stalked around a group of women chattering excitedly over a window display, and blinked at the sight of a familiar woman sitting on a bench. He froze, completely stunned, as Karenna Digby spotted him, tossed him a brilliant smile and rose from the bench with Matthew gurgling in her arms.

What was *she* doing with the boy?

Chapter Four

Karenna saw the big, powerful man wade through the crowd on the sidewalk like he was marching through a river with confidence and steel. His gaze on her didn't waver. A few women definitely threw him interested looks, but he didn't notice. Although the bright sun washed over him, he could be walking in shadows.

A few paces brought him close enough for her to see the banked fire in his eyes and the tension snapping in the muscles of his jaw. Matthew squirmed in her arms, burying more deeply against her. She realized, as Gage skidded to an imposing stop in front of her, that the fire wasn't anger but concern for the child.

"I told your grandmother to go to her church meeting," she explained, gently patting Matthew's little back. "She confessed she'd been missing her friends and the fellowship, so I'm doing some shopping, and Matthew, the gentleman that he is, has agreed to accompany me."

A muscle jumped along Gage's right temple. She wouldn't have been surprised to see steam coming out of his ears. His gaze fell to the bench where a few shopping bags sat waiting for her. He probably had some preconceived notion about women who shopped.

"Gran left you alone with the baby?" He bit it out, bulking up like a bear in a rage.

"Why shouldn't she? I'm a licensed day-care worker, not in the state of Alaska, but still, I'm more than capable." The baby cooed, his fists clinging to her T-shirt, holding on.

Poor little guy. She gently tugged one plump baby fist free and gave his knuckles a raspberry kiss, earning a bubbly grin and a shout of glee. Matthew tried to keep her captive with his gaze.

She tweaked his nose playfully, earning an ear-to-ear smile, before turning her attention to the glowering man who didn't look happy at all.

"What? Jean appreciated the offer. She hasn't been able to enjoy her friends and church activities as much since Matthew came to stay." She was not intimidated by the mountain man, and now that she knew what to look for, she could see the hurt. That was the reason for the barrier he kept up between people, and the way he pushed at her to keep a safe distance between them.

Having been recently rejected by the man she loved, she understood, so she gentled her voice. "I'm not faulting you. I'm just wondering about Matthew's mother. I don't know the situation, but surely she would want to lend a hand?"

"Wendy died giving birth to him." Flatly said, without a hint of sorrow. Surely it had to be there, but it was impossible to see.

"I didn't know." Horrified, she fell silent, her gaze drifting to the baby grinning up at her, blowing bubbles. He gave another gleeful holler, pleased at the level of noise he was capable of. Several passersby on the street smiled at his cute efforts. Carefully, she gathered the right words. What Gage must think of her! "I'm sorry. I'm always putting my foot in my mouth. I have a knack for saying just the wrong thing."

"I've noticed." A muscle twitched in his jaw, the only sign of emotion. He didn't look like an architect in wash-worn jeans, an untucked, unbuttoned flannel shirt and a T-shirt advertising the tour company he worked for. But if she imagined him in a suit and tie, well... *wow.* That was the only word that came to mind. And the even more amazing thing about Gage Parker was the compassion on his face, the honest sympathy for his nephew that proved he wasn't made of stone after all.

"Poor Matthew." She gave the baby a gentle stroke along the crown of his downy head. What a sad situation, but because of Gage, Matthew had a safe and loving home. Gage was much more of a man than he portrayed. "It can't be an easy situation for any of you."

"No, but we're all managing." Tendons hardened in his neck, hinting that his emotion went deeper and truer than he felt comfortable showing. "What about you? Don't tell me we're stuck with you for another night."

"Sorry, but no." She scooped up the handles of her shopping bags with her free hand. "Jean found a place for me to stay. The reverend and his wife have offered me their guest bedroom. Isn't that nice? At least I have a roof over my head while I consider my options."

"Options?" He glowered. "What options?"

"There you go, always expecting the worst." She watched furrows dig deeper into his intelligent forehead. With the controlled male power radiating from him, she could picture him designing buildings and taking meetings. He definitely was the kind of man who would succeed anywhere. His wounded heart would heal one day, and then he would be a real catch for the right woman. Not her—but the right woman.

"It isn't like I can drive back to Seattle without a working car." She wanted to enter the diner, but between the crowds and the bench he blocked her way. "Excuse me."

"What about a plane?" He took one step over to let her pass, hulking over her. "We have airlines and airports in Alaska. Surprise. You could fly home."

"I could." She waltzed by him. "What about my car? I can't leave it here."

"Because that would be a tragedy?"

"Yes." A smile twitched at the corners of her mouth. Who knew the rumors were true? The mountain man *was* hiding a sense of humor. He might not be laughing now—not with that scowl on his face—but she caught a glimpse of something deeper—and that was really attractive. Not that she should be noticing. "I need my car so I can find a new apartment and a new job."

"What happened to your old ones?"

"I was getting married, remember?" She tried shifting her shopping bags so she could open the door, but Gage got there first. Determined not to be affected by his presence, she sailed through the door he held open, and into the diner. "I had a plan all mapped out. I was going to move into Alan's condo. I couldn't get time off for my honeymoon, so I was forced to give notice. Alan was going to take me on a month-long cruise."

"I suppose that's where he is?"

"That's my guess, too." A lock of hair tumbled over her shoulder, hiding her face as she grabbed a high chair from against the wall.

"Let me do that." He scooted her aside and grabbed

the chair. He didn't like being seen with her on the street and not in the diner. He did his best to ignore several curious stares as he followed her to an available table, but he couldn't walk away. He might not know what to do with the boy, but he was responsible for him. He set the chair in place.

"Thanks." She beamed, making his pulse catch.

Each time she smiled, she became impossibly prettier. Another reason to dislike her. He stepped back, watching as she slid the baby into the chair and buckled him in safely. She did seem very caring. Her touch was as gentle as her voice. Matthew gazed up at her, transfixed.

"It was decent of you to give Gran the afternoon off." He reluctantly eased onto the bench across from her. "Thanks for that."

"Jean has been so nice to me. She lent me some clothes and took me into town to buy new outfits, since Alan didn't load my luggage into the back of my car like I asked. Then she introduced me to the reverend and his wife." She stopped to give the waitress her drink order—a soda.

It sounded good, so he did the same.

"Gran did all that for you?" he asked, when the waitress was gone.

"Yes. Jean is marvelous. I'm totally in love with her." She tore the paper off her straw and plunked it into her cup. "See? Good has already come out of this trip. I've made new friends. Who knows what else awaits me here? Surely good things can happen in this beautiful place."

"It is beautiful." He couldn't argue there. She captivated him like a fairy-tale princess come to life, sweeping into his life as if she were part of some story realm.

The pink shirt and jeans she wore looked sensible and casual, but there was something extraordinary about her as she dug a bottle out of Matthew's diaper bag, uncapped it and held it for him. Her graceful movements and the contented love on her face as she tended the boy were captivating.

"So, Gage, can we be friends now?"

"Whoa, I didn't say anything about being friendly." He held up his hands helplessly, blushing a little because he realized he'd been staring. Embarrassed by that, and a little shocked, he pulled his soda closer and took a sip. "I have a no-friends policy when it comes to women."

"You wouldn't be interested in making an exception?" Her question was warm, not accusing. "I'm not so bad, once you get to know me."

"I've seen you in action. Kicking the car. You have a temper."

"Sometimes." Her laughter rang like a merry bell. "Mostly, I hardly ever kick stuff."

"What a relief." Was he grinning ear to ear? Probably. He shifted in the booth, hoping he didn't look as if he were enjoying her company. "As long as your temper is under control, we *could* be acquaintances."

"I'll settle for that, but you're still worried. Admit it." She searched through her menu and peered at him over the upper edge. "You think you're in danger from me because I'm on a husband hunt."

"Aren't you?"

"Sure, but I want the right guy, and no offense, but you're not him."

"Ouch."

"Sorry." She studied the menu, fighting a smile. "I'm looking for someone more, well, agreeable."

"You're looking for more than that." He ought to be

relieved, but he wasn't. Instead, the tension in his gut worsened. "Go ahead and admit it. You have a whole laundry list of fine qualities you're looking for in a man."

"Sure. I want someone who matches me, someone I can go through life with. I'm looking for the perfect guy."

Why did Bucky come to mind? Gage flipped open his menu with an angry snap. What was this sharp, blazing sensation axing into his chest? Indigestion? Starvation? The first signs of a heart attack? "Perfect is overrated."

"No, it isn't. It's what everyone is looking for." She set the menu down and took a delicate sip of her soda. "I mean, don't you have this picture in your mind of the exact right person for you?"

"No." There was no woman right for him. He'd learned that the hard way. He was too stubborn and too disenchanted to believe otherwise. He stared intently at the menu, the black print meaningless.

"Maybe it's a girl thing." She pulled a small cloth from the diaper bag and wiped Matthew's chin. He blew bubbles, his bottle forgotten. "Romance is a big deal to us. Weddings are even bigger."

"No kidding." He blinked, trying to make sense of the writing on the menu. But instead, all he could think about was how Bucky wanted to take a crack at Karenna. Instead of the list of home-cooked specials, all he could see was Bucky's youthful charm. Karenna's perfect match.

The blazing, piercing sensation hitting like a pickax against his sternum wasn't indigestion, it was jealousy.

He didn't normally consider himself a jealous man,

so why today? Why her? He was *not* interested in the
woman. Everything about her was wrong, from her
cheerfulness to her domestic skills.

Now he felt like a fool. He was all worked up over
Karenna and Bucky, and they hadn't been on a single
date. Boy, was he in trouble.

What was going on with him? He was a mess. He
swiped beaded sweat from his brow, opened his mouth
a few times to work out the kinks in his knotted-up jaw
muscles and was relieved when the waitress returned
for their order.

"I'm waiting for Jean," Karenna explained, and the
waitress seemed good with that.

He wasn't. How was he going to sit here minute after
minute, battling down jealousy and emotions he didn't
want to understand? The woman across the table from
him lifted the baby into her arms and spoke softly. She
made a pretty picture, with the sunlight falling like
liquid gold against her hair. She was poetry in his rough-
and-tumble living room—she was like a dream that
vanished when morning came and a man opened his
eyes.

"That's a good boy." She settled the baby in her arms.
There was no doubt Matthew responded well to her.
He'd been fussy ever since he arrived—correct that,
ever since he'd been abandoned without explanation.

"I can see you were good at your job." He flipped
the menu shut. "You have a real way with babies."

"There's no secret to it. Babies respond to love." She
smiled up at him. Not one of those bright, cheerful
smiles, but one he'd never seen before. A thoughtful one
that showed her quiet, sensitive nature. Exactly the kind
of woman he was looking for—correct that!—*wasn't*
looking for.

She jerked her gaze from his, and the moment shattered. Suddenly she looked uncomfortable and far too busy, holding Matthew's bottle for him.

He wasn't the only one uncomfortable, he realized, watching the content baby cuddled against her. He looked like one happy baby.

Gage's emotions reeled, and his head spun. "So, you're planning on staying in town for a while?"

"That's why I drove to Alaska. It's time for a new adventure in my life." Her words were cheerful and optimistic, but something had changed. He could see beyond her smile to a deeper pain she kept hidden.

"Being left at the altar must have hurt pretty bad." He wasn't a sensitive man by any stretch, but he could put himself in her shoes. "Rejection hurts. I'm sure it's worse when it happens in front of the people you care about."

"It was crushing." Her chin bobbed just a bit, a hint at how hard she was working to stay in control of her emotions.

He had to credit her for that. Maybe she was a good woman, as far as women went. She might be impressionable and unrealistic, but those things were not crimes and, heaven knew, there were worse things to be. He could use some of that around his house. A helping hand, a sunny disposition and comforting friendship for Gran.

Don't even think it, he told himself, but the words tumbled out anyway. "You know I've been looking for a nanny for Matthew."

"Yes, you mentioned it."

He put his napkin in his lap, doing his best to ignore the crazy hammering of his pulse and the falling pit in his stomach. A sure sign of doom, but he asked the question anyway. "Would you consider taking the job?"

Seconds turned into an eternity as she stared at him, her rosebud mouth slightly agape. Her surprise couldn't be more obvious. If he had suddenly grown another head and sprouted antennae, he didn't think he could have shocked her more.

"I mean, you may not be interested." He swallowed. Maybe he ought to be fully honest here. "But it would be a help to my grandmother and a burden off my mind. Just think about it."

She nodded, her gaze traveling to the window, where, outside, a gray Subaru crept into a free parking space. Hard not to recognize Gran behind the wheel. Looked like she'd come just in time to rescue him.

"Let's not say anything to her just yet." The pit in his stomach seemed to widen. Definitely a sign to him that this was a bad idea, but did he take back his offer? He couldn't. Gran needed help, and Matthew loved Karenna. He didn't have a better choice. "I don't want to get her hopes up just yet, until you decide."

Karenna nodded, her golden curls bouncing slightly as she gazed down at the boy. When she smiled at Matthew and smoothed the curve of her hand over his soft hair, there was no mistaking the way the baby lit up with contentment.

What was he going to do if she said yes? It would be a good decision for Matthew and for Gran, but not for him. He rose from the table to open the diner's door for his grandmother.

"That was sure some supper you treated us to," Jean said, as she handed Karenna her cardigan sweater from one of the shopping bags.

"It was my pleasure." How could it not be? Jean and little Matthew's company today had lifted her spirits, when they'd been sorely hurting. Karenna slipped into the soft garment and grabbed her purse and other shopping bags. "This is totally the nicest evening I've had in a long time."

"I enjoyed it, too, dear." Jean looked pleased as she walked through the door her grandson held, amusement wreathing her face. "Look at Gage, foaming at the mouth to get going. Can't blame him. He's got work in the morning. He's taken over more of the tours since poor Ben died."

"I read about that in the article." Karenna did her best not to react when she slid past Gage and onto the sidewalk. "Ben had a wife and sons?"

"Two adorable little guys. Amy was destroyed, of course. She had a good husband in that man. Ben was a friend of Gage's, did you know? Not just his boss. When he died, the tour company nearly went under. The whole town suffered because of it."

"I see." It was an eternity ago, or so it seemed, when she'd been sitting in the Bellingham diner studying the *Now Woman* article. She'd been carried away by the idea of all the handsome, hunky single men in one town. Now she saw another angle, a deeper one—an innocent life lost, a family broken, the company struggling. "I'm so sorry. This is a small town, it must be close-knit. One man's loss has to be deeply felt."

"That it is." Jean wrapped her in an one-armed hug, careful of the baby she held, and clung tight for a moment, holding on. When she let go, emotion teared her eyes. "I hope we meet up real soon, Karenna. You have been a godsend. I'm sure you'll be busy getting acquainted around and whatnot, but maybe we could have lunch here at the diner sometime. I could bring Matthew."

"That sounds perfect. I would love it." She had a hard time forcing her feet to carry her away from Jean. "Good night."

"Dear, you go easy on poor Gage. If he keeps scowling like that, his face is going to stay that way."

Karenna stepped into the temperate evening breezes, considering the man who stood with both arms crossed over his burly chest, leaning against the side of his Jeep, the passenger door open and a frown on his face. Impossible to miss that grimace from a mile away.

"Too late. It's already happened." She couldn't resist teasing, especially because she knew he could hear them. His scowl deepened, but perhaps that was for show, since there was also a glint of trouble in his eyes.

"I don't appreciate you siding with my grandmother." He looked serious as he caught her elbow and helped her onto the seat, but the corners of his mouth were trying to curve upward. Maybe he didn't mind that his grandmother had volunteered him to see her to the Michaelses.

"A big, tough guy like you should be able to take it." She buckled up, noticing just how attractive Gage was. He wasn't as guarded, and the planes of his face had softened. He no longer looked like the bitter Sasquatch kind of guy she'd first met. No, he was all-American, all decency and male appeal.

"I'm beginning to regret offering you the job."

"Too bad, because I'm going to take it."

"You are?" He shut the door. "I was sure you were going to turn me down."

"Why?"

"Because you're looking for a husband. Taking care of a baby all day is bound to slow you down."

"I like slow." He could tease, she could tease. "Besides, this will give me something to do while I scope out potential grooms. I brought a tux with me. I just need the right man to fit it, and I'm good to go."

"You're kidding, right?" He crooked one brow, only enhancing his good looks.

"Me, kidding?" She winked at him. "I'll never tell."

He *almost* cracked a smile. He shook his head, turned on his heels and circled to the front of the Jeep, giving her a most excellent view.

Not that she was into him, but she wasn't dead. A girl could appreciate a very attractive man, even if he wasn't right for her.

Okay, he couldn't be more *wrong* for her, but still....

She ripped her gaze from him, sat straighter in the seat and placed her purse and shopping bags on the floor. It was going to be interesting having a hunk for a boss.

Chapter Five

"Seven o'clock tomorrow morning," Gage agreed, as he pulled his rig to a stop in Reverend Michaels's driveway. Curtains were drawn open on the front windows of the house, but no visual on the reverend and his wife. He was feeling good for a change. Karenna wasn't a permanent solution to his problem. She had the whole world of options to choose from, not to mention Bucky's ardent interest.

There went those hot spikes of jealousy again. He winced, shouldered open the door and hit the ground. He walked fast and hard trying to escape it, but that pesky emotion stayed with him like his shadow. By the time he'd reached the passenger door, Karenna had already swung it open. He had time to grab her before she hopped out of the vehicle. Her skin was satin soft, her hand felt delicate tucked in his own. Peacefulness curled around the chunk of charcoal that had become his heart.

Strange. When he let go of her to shut the door, the emotions remained. He took a step beside her, intent on walking her to the front door, and the peacefulness stuck with him, washing out the flare of jealousy. It was stronger than his pessimism, tougher than his will.

"There is one problem." She waltzed beside him, as fresh as the temperate evening air, as perfect as Alaska's blue sky. Completely unaware of the emotion she'd caused. "I don't have a car."

"Then I'll come get you in the morning."

"No. That's not right. I can't expect you to do that. You have a long workday as it is. I don't want to add to it. I'll figure something out."

"It's not like you can walk all the way from town to my house."

"I'm not as helpless as you think."

"Never said you were helpless. You took amazing care of Matthew today. You made a big difference to my grandmother. That's mighty helpful, in my book." *Way to hide your feelings, Gage.* He grimaced, wondering where his growl and bark went. He was losing his edge. First mushy, peaceful feelings and now this. What would happen next? He did not want to find out.

"I'm glad. Did you know I love to cook? It's a great love of mine. I insisted on making a casserole to freeze before we left the house. What? Don't make that face. I'm a good cook."

"I'm not so bad in the kitchen myself." Why he confessed such a thing, he didn't know. Wasn't he supposed to be putting distance between them? Keeping his gruff image? Making it clear they weren't friends, that in fact, they would never be more than tolerable acquaintances?

"I don't believe it. Not without proof." She scanned him up and down, mirth playing across her features. In the gentle light she was transformed, more beautiful than anything he'd ever set eyes on. She tripped up the steps, willowy and light, and spun to face him. "Nope, I can't see you as a master of the kitchen."

"What does that mean? You *can* see me burning dinner? Scorching potatoes? Overcooking a steak?"

"I can't picture you doing anything domestic." She tilted her head a tad, enough so that her golden hair tumbled over her slender shoulders, exposing the sculpted line of her cheek and jaw. Such a dear face she had.

He fell silent, his pulse skidded to a halt and the ribbon of emotion around his cold heart tugged one notch looser.

"You are mountain-man tough," she said, gently kidding. "I can see you working for the tour company. I'm sure you are one of their finest guides. I can picture you doing all kinds of masculine things around the house, like chopping down trees, riding a motorcycle, climbing a mountain. I can't see you whipping up a crème brûlée."

"Desserts aren't my specialty." Why was he bantering with her? Why did he want to make her smile one more time, and just for him? "I can make an excellent pan of brownies."

"You tell a good joke, Gage." She laughed, a little trill of joy, and she laid the flat of her hand against the plane of his chest. A light gesture, nothing significant, but he felt it like a hook to his spirit.

Heaven help him, because his gaze arrowed to her mouth—to her rosebud smile. Her full-of-life radiance drew him. He wanted to kiss her, he realized with a shake of his head. What a crazy, dumb, reckless thing to want. He froze on the porch step, with his knees weak and loneliness strangling him, stuggling between the wish to step forward and the need for self-preservation and distance.

You don't want to get personal with the girl, he reminded himself. There were a whole host of reasons, the least of which was his fear of relationships. He felt the grin fade from his face and the weariness return to his hibernating heart. "I'll see you in the morning?"

"Yes. And I'm looking forward to being Matthew's nanny." She laid her hand on his wrist, a friendly gesture, nothing more. Her incredible blue eyes searched his, bright with happiness. "I had a lovely evening with you, Gage. Thank you."

Yes, he could see she meant that, and it made him uneasy. Her hand was soft on his arm, a connection he did not invite or want. He had to do something about that now. Make his wishes clear. Set and defend his boundaries.

He broke away from her touch, maybe a little too harshly. He focused on the porch board at his feet, so he wouldn't have to look at her and see the consequences of what he'd done on her stunning face.

"Matthew is the one who needs you." His voice sounded cold. It couldn't be helped. It was who he was. She might as well get that figured out now. All the cheer in the world couldn't save him. "He's the one counting on you."

"I know." Confusion layered her words. "I promise to take the best care of him. He deserves nothing less."

"As long as we're in agreement." He had to unclamp his jaw enough to speak. He didn't know what was wrong with him. He couldn't say why he was so mad. Okay, not mad exactly. Just upset and twisted inside out. He retreated down the walkway without wishing her a good night.

She said nothing either, standing in the sweep of the porch light, looking so alone and forlorn he had to walk

faster to keep ahead of the emotion threatening to pull
him back and take him under.

Don't start caring about her, he told himself, as a
raindrop landed on his nose. Another hit his cheek. The
only warning before a torrent hit. The skies opened up
and thunder crashed across the sky.

Alone, and forlorn, too, he hopped in his Jeep and
drove away. But he checked his rearview to make sure
the Michaelses' front door opened and Karenna disappeared safely inside.

What was up with Gage? That question haunted her
through the hour or so it had taken to get settled into
the Michaelses' guest room. He'd gone from charming to granite in ten seconds flat. And she thought she
knew why. She'd reached out to him, she'd made that
comment about having a lovely evening with him, and
he'd probably taken it the wrong way. He'd been perfectly clear from the beginning about what he thought
of marriage-minded women. What had he told her the
first night she'd met him?

That's right. He'd told her in no uncertain terms he
was off the market and would tolerate no funny stuff,
which meant flirting. Surely he didn't think she had
been flirting with him? She unzipped the little toiletries
bag she'd picked up in the local general store and carried
it into the adjoining bathroom. One look in the mirror
knocked the air from her lungs. She didn't recognize
herself.

Sure, the face was hers, and so were the blond curls
and the five extra pounds she hadn't been able to lose
before the wedding. It was her eyes that shocked her,
heavy and shadowed as they were, with sadness she
could not keep hidden. She totally did not want to feel

the heartbreak she'd driven so far to get away from, but there it was, looking at her back in the mirror.

An electronic chime broke the silence and startled her out of her thoughts. She had cell service? Yay. She hadn't thought to check her phone in town. She raced to the bed where she'd tossed her purse, and dug into it. She recognized the number—her cousin was calling. Her fingers trembled as she answered the call. "Maryann?"

"Karenna. What a relief." The voice on the other end of the line sounded frayed. "I was about to file a missing persons report on you. It's been days and days since you drove away from the church without a single word."

"I know. I'm sorry." She thought of all that had happened—her car breaking down, Gage rescuing her at the roadside, spending the night with the family and then discovering the town with Matthew in the afternoon. Gage's presence still affected her. "I just forgot to call."

"Only you could forget to check in. Didn't you think your family might be worried about you?"

"Disappointed, maybe." She thought of her sisters and her mom, who had seemed to empathize with Alan. How did she explain she'd been first too upset and then too humiliated to call? "I didn't mean to worry anyone."

"We are worrying, believe me. You could have contacted someone."

"I know, but with every passing mile it became harder to pick up the phone. I don't know what to say, except that I messed things up. Again."

"Where are you? The reception is terrible. I can hardly hear you."

"In Alaska."

"Sorry, I must have misheard you. It sounded as if you said Alaska."

"I did." Here it came—the judgment. She loved Maryann dearly, but her cousin was a confirmed bachelorette. Braced for the worst, Karenna zipped her suitcase. "There's this article in *Now Woman* magazine—"

"You didn't!" Maryann sounded aghast. "Not that ridiculous story about men needing wives in some small town—"

"Treasure Creek," she supplied.

"You *did* read it! You *are* there."

"Maryann, I'm totally shocked you even know about it." She sat on the edge of the bed, delighted. Was her antimarriage cousin experiencing a change in attitude? "You read the article, too?"

"No, but it's all anyone on my floor is talking about." Maryann was a nurse in California. "It sounds like nonsense to me. I can't believe you drove that distance by yourself, chasing after some fairy-tale story."

"It's not a fairy tale. There are some really nice bachelors here. Are you going to come check out the hunks, too?"

"Are you crazy? Why would I want to? I certainly don't need to have a man to be happy." Maryann's favorite refrain. "The other nurses in the lunchroom were talking about taking vacation time for a trip up there, but it sounds foolish to me."

"Not foolish. Romantic."

"Nonsense. You don't sound like yourself, Karenna." Maryann could be tough, but she was deeply caring. "You are coming home, aren't you?"

"No way. I've got a job and a place to live. I might stay up here indefinitely."

"What? Next you will be telling me you've gone and married some stranger."

"Not yet, but you never know." Why Gage's handsome face popped into her mind was a mystery. There was something compelling about him. He was confident and stalwart and carried a deep wound.

Not that he was right for her, not that she was interested in marrying him—can you imagine?—but he'd been sweet to her tonight, getting her a chair, opening and closing her doors, helping her in and out of the Jeep. He was a real gentleman, the genuine article. A girl didn't run into that every day. Why shouldn't she admire him? There was nothing wrong with that.

"You're making a mistake." Maryann, bless her, sounded so sure of herself. "You're going to leap with both feet into a worse situation."

"I know you mean well, but I'm fine."

"How can you be? What Alan did to you was atrocious. But you have to see that coming home is the best thing for you right now. You're not thinking clearly."

"My head has never been clearer." She began unpacking things from her shopping bags, sorting them on the bed.

"Maybe I ought to come up there myself and talk some sense into you."

"I know you mean well, but you're concerned over nothing." Static crackled in her ear. It really was a bad connection. Wait—there was only silence. That wasn't right. "Maryann?"

Nothing.

She'd lost the call and the signal. Knowing Maryann, she would call back after she calmed down. Maybe she would be easier to talk to then.

She wasn't going to sink into a depression over Alan.

She caught her reflection in the dresser mirror, hiked up her chin and tried to put a smile on her face. She squinted at herself, disappointed the upturn of her mouth didn't look genuine. It didn't chase the pain from her eyes or from her heart.

She'd woven dreams into their years together, as they'd held hands walking through the arboretum or along Green Lake. She would ask him to stop at open houses with the for sale signs swinging in the yard and they would walk the rooms, imagining the life they would have one day, for the children to come.

He'd been ripped out of her life suddenly. One moment, she was waiting with breathless joy in the church's vestibule, then the next he was gone. There was only a void where he'd been, only a crushing pain where his love used to be. Seven long years he had filled her life. Maryann's call brought it all speeding back.

She opened her purse and dug into a zippered compartment until the cool platinum brushed her fingers. She fished out the engagement ring, remembering how Alan had knelt before her in front of the Christmas tree at her parent's house. She'd been hoping for a proposal. Joy had rushed through her—Alan wanted her. With her entire family watching, he'd asked her to be his wife.

Her mother had answered for her, shouting, "Yes! Say yes, Karenna!" before she could form the words.

The diamond winked up at her, a sign of broken promises.

Be honest, she ordered. You are hoping that Alan will call. That he had some entirely understandable reason for abandoning her. That he wanted her back.

What if he'd been her only chance for happiness? She tucked the diamond back into her purse. When she had time, she would package it up and overnight it to him, to the man who hadn't loved her enough.

What if no man would? The secret fear inside her intensified. She wished she was more like Maryann, confident of her singleness and proud of it. She wished she could say, "too bad for Alan, he made the worst decision of his life." She hated the part of her that pined for him, because while their romance hadn't been dazzling emotions and grand gestures, it had been comfortable and companionable and comforting.

Now it was gone. Could she ever find that again? The silence around her resonated with the sorrow she'd been avoiding since her brother-in-law handed her Alan's letter in the church sanctuary. There was no place to run, no way to distract herself from the failure battering her. No way to hide from her sadness.

What would Gage think if he could see her now, she wondered? She thought about the man who always used to laugh. She understood how deep a love's loss could rip into a person—that, while she and Alan had not been husband and wife, seven years together of friendship and memories, of togetherness and woven dreams was a lot to lose.

The emotions weighing on her spirit felt terribly dark. She thought of Gage and his bitterness. That was how he coped, she realized. He put up a wall of bitterness around him to protect himself from being hurt like that again, which meant he intended to keep away anyone who might be able to love him. He meant to never love again.

She could see how tempting that would be. In truth, she never wanted to feel this way. But shutting out life was not what she wanted. How did she put aside her fears and her failures? How did she start over again, when her life had taken such an abrupt and irrevocable turn?

There was only one place to go. She found her Bible, stroked the worn leather cover and leafed through the gossamer-thin pages. She'd marked dozens upon dozens of pages over the years, made notes in the margins and highlighted passages in bold colors—yellow, orange, green. She flipped through the treasured verses until the right one from Jeremiah caught her eye. *For I know the plans I have for you,* says the Lord. *They are plans for good and not for disaster, to give you a future and a hope.*

Believe, she told herself. *Just believe.* God was with her now, and He would help her.

Please, let me find a place to belong, she prayed. With someone who accepted her as she was. This time with someone who would never let her down.

It was a tall order, and she didn't know if it was possible. Loneliness crept into her soul when she imagined her future without someone to love.

And, no—she made sure every image of Gage Parker stayed completely out of her mind. She didn't let in the slightest picture, the tiniest hint.

A knock sounded on her door. "Karenna?" It was the reverend's wife, Jenny. "Did you want to come have some pie with us? I have homemade ice cream to go with it."

"Yes, I would love to." She cleared the emotion from her throat and opened the door.

Chapter Six

The next morning as Gage got ready to leave for work, Karenna was still on his mind. That didn't make him happy. Last night had been too close for his comfort. It had troubled him enough to interrupt his sleep, and he wasn't in the best of moods because of it. He knew he was scowling when his grandmother scuffled into the room. He tried to stop, but the muscles in his face felt stuck in place.

"Goodness! What's with you?" Gran had Matthew on her arm, the little guy blinking as if he wasn't sure if he wanted to be asleep or awake. "For a moment there, I thought a bear was in my kitchen."

"Funny." Except he still couldn't make the scowl go away. He felt the muscles pucker in his forehead, but would they relax?

No. And he knew why.

"Let's pray that Karenna gets here after you head off for work." Gran shook her head as she settled the baby into his high chair. "Because if she gets a look at you like that, she'll change her mind lickety-split and refuse to work for us."

"No need to worry." He grumbled as he spun the thermos lid tight and headed toward the door. "I'm outta here."

"I hope your day improves, dear." His grandmother was busy buckling in the baby, but she had time to cast him a schoolmarm look, the one that said he'd best straighten up or else.

If only he could.

"And thanks for hiring dear Karenna," Gran called after him. "You've made my day, boy."

That was the upside of a very bad idea. He yanked open the back door, not looking forward to the prospect of a staff meeting. He would rather be outside in the fresh air. Although it was a toss-up as to whether he wanted to be out on the river this afternoon with another bunch of marriage-crazy women. What happened to his quiet, sedate life?

A terrible pain knifed through his temples as he shouldered past the screen door, a clue that it was going to be one of those days. He thumped down the steps. At least the upside was that he'd been successfully able to avoid Karenna. No sign of her yet.

Hold on. It sounded like someone was coming down the driveway. Tires scattering gravel and a big engine's rumbling had him hiking as fast as he could go to his rig. It might be late to avoid her, but maybe he could minimize the time spent with her. That would make last night a whole lot easier to forget. He hoped she would table her unreasonable idea that they could be friends.

He'd reached the garage by the time the tow truck ground to a halt in the driveway. One look at Bucky grinning ear to ear behind the wheel made the knife in his temple feel like a machete.

Good, he told himself. *I ought to be ecstatic. The*

fairy-tale princess and the golden boy are together.
They are the perfect match, and I'm off the hook.

It was a relief.

So why did the muscles in his forehead tug so tight that it felt as if his hair follicles were creeping over the top of his head?

"'Mornin', Gage!" The golden boy hopped out of his truck, his white smile so bright, he could temporarily blind someone. "Look who I found on the road from town?"

"Hi, Gage." Karenna hadn't waited for her prince to open her door. She popped into sight around the front of the rig with a backpack slung over one shoulder. "I tried to be here early enough to see you off to work."

She looked so happy about being the good employee, how could he tell her he'd left a little early this morning to avoid her?

Last night continued to trouble him. He could feel the pull of their remembered closeness. His arm tingled pleasantly where her hand had been, an innocent reminder of her offer of friendship and all the reasons why he couldn't accept it.

He kept his scowl in place. "Got to get goin'. Gran is in the kitchen with Matthew."

"I should get in to help her." Karenna hiked her pack higher on her shoulder. "I hope you have a good day."

"You, too." He could barely get the words out. His throat had suddenly gone dry and felt thick, as if he'd swallowed a jar of peanut butter.

He hopped into his Jeep, jammed the keys into the ignition and the engine caught. But he couldn't go anywhere because the tow truck blocked him in. Worse, he had a bird's eye view of Bucky rolling an old red bicycle up to the porch and leaning it against the rails.

He looked like a courtin' man, shoulders straight, chest puffed out, all his senses focused on the petite, golden-haired lady who thanked him with a muted smile.

The couple exchanged words. He could guess what they were saying—courting talk. Bucky uttered something, earning a ripple of laughter and a tilt of her head. She looked glorious with the breeze in her hair, the sun highlighting her like a promise. Even in a simple zip-up sweatshirt, a pink T-shirt and jeans, she looked remarkable, as if she'd strolled off the pages of a magazine advertising everything upright in the world.

He gritted his teeth, fisted his hands around the wheel and refused to let jealousy touch him again. *That* would be a mistake.

"Sorry, Gage!" Bucky jogged over after waving goodbye to Karenna. "Didn't mean to hold you up."

"I know." Karenna had a way of drawing a man in until he forgot the world existed. He knew from first-hand experience. He followed Bucky down the driveway, doing his best not to give Karenna another thought.

"Did Gage seem okay to you?" Karenna poured two cups of coffee, watching Jean's reaction.

"He was wearing his big scowl today." The older woman propped her hands on the table and stood. "Don't know what got into his craw this morning. There's no telling with him."

"I hope it's not over me being here." She settled the pot back onto the coffeemaker.

"I would have said it had something to do with Bucky, but Gage was in a mood long before you arrived in that tow truck." Jean's eyes twinkled. "Anything goin' on there?"

"With Bucky? No. Heavens *no,*" she emphasized, set

the plates on the table and twirled on her sneakers to grab the fruit from the refrigerator. "I'm not interested in the tow truck guy."

"Not even a little? He sure seemed interested in you."

"He was being nice is all." Karenna rescued the bowl of berries she'd washed from the shelf and two steaming bowls of hot cereal from the counter. She wanted to like Bucky. He definitely fit the bill for Mr. Right. So why didn't she feel something for him? "He came across me biking and offered me a ride. I wasn't sure how long it would take me to get here, so I agreed. I didn't want to be late. That's all there was to it. Now, this is steel-cut oatmeal. Be sure and eat it all. It's good for your blood sugar."

"I miss my powdered doughnuts." Jean wrinkled her nose. "Sure I can't put some sugar on this?"

"Try the fruit. It will be better for you."

"I know it, I just don't like it. You're a dear for caring. Now, back to Bucky. Are you sure you don't find him attractive?"

"I'm positive." She slid into the chair across from Jean, trying to conjure up a picture of the tow truck guy and couldn't do it. But Gage came to mind—only Gage. Gage, looking like he'd walked off some rugged movie set, with his tousled dark hair, a days' growth shadowing his jaw and a world-weary attitude.

A tiny sigh escaped her. A total accident. She wasn't interested in the man, although he was possibly the most handsome one she'd ever laid eyes on. Matthew chose that moment to kick in his high chair and she turned to tweak his nose. "Last night when Gage took me to the reverend's, I think I gave him the wrong impression."

"What impression would that be?" Jean unfolded her paper napkin and placed it on her lap.

"That I was flirting with him." She didn't merely blush. Her face turned flaming red. She could see the tip of her nose gleaming like a ripe strawberry.

"Flirting? I'm sure Gage didn't think anything untoward."

"He became upset with me. I was only meaning to be friendly." She snared a napkin from the holder. "He doesn't have any women friends?"

"No. The only women he trusts are me and his boss, Amy James. Other than that, Gage won't have anything to do with a woman. I'm frankly shocked he agreed to hire you." Jean clasped her hands, ready for the blessing. "Don't you worry none. He isn't a hard man. Whatever went on between you two last night, he wouldn't have reacted if he didn't care. Do you want to say grace, dear?"

"You do the honor." She clasped her hands and bowed her head, content to listen to Jean's warbling voice as she thanked the Lord for their blessings and asked for guidance.

Please help me make things right with Gage, she added, silently. She liked this job, and she didn't want any problems or uneasy feelings between them. She wanted Gage to think well of her. It was a matter of pride and dignity.

Or maybe it was something else best left unexamined.

Gage's vow not to give Karenna another thought was an utter failure. By the time he'd reached town, she had taken over his thoughts completely. No sense even trying to stop it.

Treasure Creek was busy, the sidewalks brimming and the shops along the town's only main road looked as if they were doing a brisk business. He squeezed into the last parking spot in the lot, beside the cozy log building that served as the company office. He unbuckled the seat belt and ambled up the sidewalk to the office's closest door.

Rachel, the receptionist, smiled when she looked up from her desk.

"You wouldn't believe the stack of messages I have for you," she sang, handing over an impressive pile of pink call-back slips. "I can't ever remember the phones being this busy."

"Lucky me." He glanced through the messages. It looked like some were from out-of-town reporters and interested folks with questions about the different tours he led. More than a few messages were from women asking about some of the handsome guides featured in the *Now Woman* article—not that he qualified for that. He frowned. The last thing he needed was to deal with more women. He handed back those messages. "Pawn those off on someone else."

Rachel laughed as if she thought he was hilarious.

He kept going. Low, gray cubicles separated one desk from another, and everyone was milling around in the aisles, sporting cups of coffee or tea. Cheerful photographs from long ago, advertising campaigns Ben had commissioned, added color to the walls. Amy was asking everyone to gather around, looking more like the woman she used to be before she lost her beloved Ben. Dr. Alex Havens, a part-time guide, asked about her little boys.

"They're fine—more than fine." She shrugged out of her light jacket. "Dexter insisted on having pancakes this morning, and Sammy wanted me to make faces on them."

Gage made a beeline toward the coffeemaker.

"Oh, my boys loved that when they were little, too," Paulette, the bookkeeper, spoke up, as she stirred sugar into her cup of coffee. "Fun times, but my little ones sure could make a mess!"

"Exactly my problem this morning. By the time the boys had decorated their pancakes, they were wearing half a quart of berries on their shirts. I don't know how they do it," Amy answered. "It was the first time Dexter wanted pancakes since he lost his daddy."

Gage remembered that Ben had been an involved father, and making pancake faces was something he and the boys always used to do. Along with dozens upon dozens of other things that they would never be able to do together again.

As he poured coffee into a ceramic cup, bleakness hit him hard. The sunshine faded from the window, as if on cue. He'd been working the day the emergency call came in that there had been an accident on the river. Ben had lost his life saving a client who had fallen into the dangerous rapids—a client who hadn't listened to his guide and cost Ben his life. Even now it choked him up.

He stirred sugar into the dark brew. His guts bunched, a sure sign of upset. He couldn't seem to stop it. His world had been off-kilter ever since he'd come across Karenna in the road.

Amy called for everyone's attention and he wandered over to his desk, taking a sip of coffee.

"Good morning." She leaned against the edge of her desk. She liked keeping things informal. "I want to start off with the good news. We are fully booked for the next six weeks."

Cheers erupted, and hope charged through the room. Gage could see it on so many faces. They were a close-knit group, and he knew everyone here was strapped, because their hours had been cut. Even the tour guides like him, who were too macho and tough to show a lick of worry. Catherine Donner, or Casey, as she liked to be called, stopped in the aisle next to him. She was one of the tour guides, too.

"I would like to add a few more tours, both river-rapid trips and overnight hikes." Amy looked hopeful. That had to be a good sign. "Paulette and I are going to start scheduling, so any guides interested in extra work, please let me know after the meeting."

A hand shot up. Nate McMann didn't wait for her acknowledgement. "We've had a lot of problems with the new women in town wandering off on their own, getting lost and stirring up trouble with local wildlife. If Gage and I get called out on search-and-rescue, are you going to be able to cover our tours?"

"Absolutely. That's why I've called everyone in, even those who have been on official lay-off. I'm going to need you all to step up and pitch in when it's needed. The good news is that everyone should be able to get plenty of hours for as long as the excitement lasts."

More cheers went up. The hope was contagious, even to him. He was generally immune to hope of all kind, at least these days, but something within him had changed.

Why and who had caused it were two questions he refused to ask himself. He did his best to turn his attention back to the meeting and the next order of business.

* * *

Bless Jean for letting her borrow the car. Karenna tucked her list of errands into her back pocket, plucked Matthew out of his car seat and shut the passenger door with her hip. It was a beautiful afternoon, and even standing on Main Street, the beauty was spectacular. The picturesque shops, the quaint, small-town feel and the majestic rise of forested mountains was everything the magazine article had promised and more. The real life experience of Treasure Creek was picture perfect. Hope lifted her heart and put a smile on her face as she faced the general store.

"Are you ready for more shopping, handsome?" she asked the little boy in her arms.

"Oh!" Matthew spoke, looking pleased with himself.

"Good boy." She kissed the downy crown of his head, settled the strap of his diaper bag higher on her shoulder and headed for the door. He was such a dear. How could his father have abandoned him? She didn't understand how anyone could have left such a dear baby. She tucked him more tightly against her, love brimming over.

"Excuse me." A petite woman with long red ringlets stopped her. She seemed friendly enough, but her very upscale designer clothes had to have been straight off Rodeo Drive. She definitely outshone the local towns-folk in jewelry alone. And her Ugg boots and high-end Alaska garb looked out of season on the sunny July day. "I just arrived here in town. Surely this isn't the only place to shop?"

"I know the choices seem limited, but I've been in the General Store before. They have a very wide variety of items." She offered a smile. "I'm Karenna."

"I'm Delilah Carrington." She flipped her designer

sunglasses off her nose, revealing cool green eyes, as she assessed the front window display. "You mean there isn't another row of shops? Another street?"

"I'm sorry. This is it." Karenna sympathized. "It's wonderful here, but being in such a small town takes some getting used to."

"I'm going to have to adapt, I suppose." Delilah bit her bottom lip. "I've decided my prince charming is here somewhere, and I intend to marry him. I just wish I had realized this place had so few shopping options."

"There's always the Internet," Karenna offered, reaching for the door.

"Yes, there is!" Delilah smiled, happy again. "I might as well follow you in and see if there's anything I want."

Judging by the black credit card she dug out of her purse, the woman wasn't in dire circumstances. But since she was on the job, Karenna said goodbye, grabbed a cart and patiently waded through the crowded store.

Boy, was it packed. Women of marriageable age were everywhere, and their excitement at being here was palpable and something she understood. Everyone had a different reason for running off to Alaska, but she suspected, like her, they were following their hearts.

"Eeee!" Matthew commented at all the excitement, grinning widely. His wide eyes sparkled with interest as he took in his surroundings.

"Here we are in the baby aisle." Karenna navigated their cart to the display of darling little clothes near the front. "Jean said you are growing like a reed. What do you think of this?"

"Oh!" Matthew studied the denim overalls very seriously.

"I agree. You will look quite handsome in this." She

plopped it into her cart and began sorting through the shirts.

"He's adorable," said a middle-aged lady standing in line nearby. She smiled sweetly at the baby who blew bubbles, quite aware of the attention. He clasped his hands together, keeping her attention. The woman appeared captivated. "How old is he?"

"Six months, but he's not mine. I'm just his nanny." Karenna chose a couple of darling T-shirts with the town's name on them.

"*Just* his nanny?" the woman questioned kindly. "Caring for a child is one of the most important jobs there is."

"True. And one of the most rewarding." Karenna couldn't help liking the woman. She had a big head of blond hair and looked to be somewhere in her forties. "Hi. I'm Karenna. Did you come because of the article, too?"

"Honey, you know I did. I'm Jolene Jones." She had an endearing smile. "Got my eye on that handsome hunk behind the counter."

Handsome? Karenna's gaze shot to the grumpy-looking man running the cash register, who also looked to be in his forties. He had a bit of a belly and didn't seem pleased at having so many dolled-up women in his store. "Good for you. He has kind eyes."

"Don't you know it. Say a prayer for me, if you don't mind, sugar. Somethin' tells me I'm gonna need a little help with that one."

"Will do." Karenna grabbed a package of blue socks from the top of the display.

"Looks like I'm next." With a wink, Jolene moved up to the counter, loaded down with purchases.

"Eee!" Matthew commented.

"That's right. We hope it works out for her." She gave him a kiss on the cheek. "Everyone deserves love."

Why did her thoughts automatically return to Gage? Whatever the reason was, it had to stop.

"Now, do you have an opinion on hats?" she asked the baby. "We need something to shade that gorgeous face of yours from the sun."

"Oh!" Matthew agreed, so she wheeled the cart deeper into the aisle, glad for the boy's sweet company.

Chapter Seven

His workday done, Gage climbed out of his Jeep, in no hurry to head up to the house. His head pounded because today his raft had been full of curious city women who'd vied for his attention. And when they hadn't been doing that, they discussed the magazine article, which had also mentioned Ben's death. Those ladies had asked all kinds of questions, curious about what happened.

Somehow, he'd managed to bite out halfway-civil answers to unaware women who did not guess he was still grieving the loss of one of his best friends, women who saw this all as a grand adventure. Well, life was no adventure, and love even less so. Couldn't they see that?

His boots dragged on the driveway and he kept his gaze on the gravel in front of his feet. He instinctively knew the sight of Karenna in his kitchen would affect him, so he put off the moment, trudging up the back steps slowly, watching his boots hit the deck boards. When he looked up, it was like being hit by lightning. She was gorgeous, like a model from a bride's magazine, with her perfect gold hair, brilliant, hopeful appearance and a song on her lips.

He ought to be able to gaze upon her now, without a single worry, because she was safely off-limits. Bucky had a claim to her. So why didn't his emotions seem to know that? If jealousy slammed into him like an out-of-control freight train, he ignored it, just as he had been doing all the day through. He took a deep breath to clear out the anger, and took another step closer to the door.

Karenna appeared to be humming as she worked at the stove, her head tilting gently with the beat. He could see her through the picture window. She moved like poetry. Every swirl of a spoon, every lift of a pot lid could have been choreographed, it was so beautiful.

She broke away from the stove with a pot's handle gripped in both hands. Still humming away, moving to the tune unconsciously, she wasn't exactly dancing, but she wasn't still, either. It reminded him of a delicate rosebud in a soft puff of an evening breeze.

Not that she affected him at all. He just couldn't help noticing her. She was like a hymn, melodic and inspiring. Any man would feel refreshed by her—she was hope on a sunny day. It was purely a platonic sort of thing. It could hardly be anything else, could it?—seeing as how she and Bucky were on the way to being an item.

The window framed Karenna as she interrupted her cooking to swoop the baby into her arms. The boy's button face beamed gleefully, and he pressed against Karenna as if he craved her affection.

Gage stopped in his tracks, emotion overtaking him. He didn't do emotions. He didn't like them or trust them. They had gotten him into a marriage that had fractured the deepest places within him. But he could not deny them now.

Karenna was the reason Matthew was happy. With all the little boy had been through—losing his mother and then Ryan's abandonment—it was a wonder the child was all right. He flourished with Karenna, obviously eating up her love and her warmth as he watched her intently, trying to keep eye contact, trying to strengthen the maternal bond he longed for.

It's a good thing she found us. The thought surprised him because it felt like a prayer, the way he used to speak to God before he'd lost hope.

Matthew needed her, and so did Gran. It was obvious Karenna would not be staying for long. The trouble was that either she would miss her life in Seattle and return, or she would find a groom—Bucky—to go along with her wedding dress.

And if jealousy bore into him again, then he ignored it. Again.

I'll do my part to keep her here. He glanced skyward, where fluffy clouds sailed on the ocean-blue sky. Matthew needed her. *Please do the rest.*

He watched as Karenna resettled the baby into the crook of one arm, brushed a kiss on his crown and returned to the stove, talking away. Whatever she said delighted the boy, because he clapped his hands together and laughed. Although Gage couldn't hear the peals, he could imagine the happy sound.

Against his will, tendrils of feeling crept around his barriers, a new tenderness he could not deny.

His decision made, he backtracked to the corner of the garage and climbed the long rise of stairs that led to the old apartment over the garage. With every step he took up the staircase, he felt the magnetic pull of her presence. Did he turn around and search for her in the windows?

No. Did he long to see her beauty and light as she sashayed with Matthew around the kitchen?

No. He kept moving, his eyes on his goal, and kicked a few errant leaves from the small deck before he gave the door a shove.

Nothing skittered when he hit the light switch. That was a good sign. At least he didn't have to chase mice or a raccoon out of the apartment. He took a tentative step in. Old pull-down shades were drawn over the windows and bars of sunshine stole around the edges, casting light into the entryway and the small corner kitchen and dining nook. While he'd never used the place as anything more than storage for Gran's furniture when she moved from her mobile home, he had considered offering it to his brother for a time. But that had been before they had quarreled, before Matthew's birth.

He doubted this was up to Karenna's standards. He frowned at the cracked linoleum at his feet and the age-worn counters. He tugged at the window blind and it jerked out of his fingers, rolling up with a sharp *snap!*

A lot of dust had settled in. It was far from upscale. He ambled into the kitchen. He turned on the sink and water flowed out. At least the plumbing was good. That was one plus.

Footsteps knelling on the stairs warned him that she was coming. So did the goose bumps skidding up his arms.

"Gage? Are you in here?" When she appeared in the door frame, it was as if she brought the sun. She stepped inside with the baby in her arms. "Oh, I had no idea this was up here. This is nice. Could use a little cleaning."

"No kidding." This morning haunted him—the way she'd smiled for Bucky, the way she'd spoken quietly with him, the way she'd made the man nearly burst with hoping. Why couldn't he get rid of that annoying jealousy?

"I was thinking of getting this place dusted and some of the boxes and furniture moved around," he told her. "This place could be habitable."

"It would bring in a good rent income for you, too. Places to live are scarce in town right now." The breeze ruffled her hair, sending it tumbling against the curve of her cheek. Nothing could be more dear than her face.

"I'm not going to rent it," he said, gruffly. "I want to fix it up."

"I could help with that."

"You?"

"Sure, why not? No need to look so panicked. I don't have any ulterior motives."

But he did. He gritted his teeth, determined to stay resistant to the melody of her voice and her contagious cheer. Especially when she flashed him the same grin she'd used on Bucky this morning. He could not forget the way the golden boy and princess had chatted together amicably, graced by the morning.

He refused to let another spear of jealousy hit him. He put on his best scowl. "It's my place, and I'll clean it myself."

"Is something wrong?" She squinted, as if trying to read the answer in his grimace.

"Why do you say that?"

"Because a bear would have a more pleasant growl." A secret thought sparkled in her eyes. "I know what's bugging you. It was all the women wanting a river tour. I've heard all about it."

"How?"

"Conversation over apple pie at the Michaelses' last night. They told me how the raft tours are in big demand because they are guided by handsome single men."

"Then it's a puzzle why I'm booked up."

"Trust me, you're handsome, Gage." She snuggled the baby to her, who added a shout of glee, as if in agreement. "You may think the scowling takes away from your appeal, but you would be wrong. Some women might go weak at the dark, mysterious, gruff mountain man thing you've got going."

"Tell me you're joking."

"Oh, I'm serious. *I'm* not one of those women, but still, you do have a certain appeal. You might want to consider frowning a little less. Those poor women in your raft were probably in a dither from your magnetic presence."

"Don't defend them. My head is still ringing from all the cackling nonsense. The chatter went on and on for most of the afternoon. I'm afraid I'll be hearing them in my sleep." He pulled another blind, and sunlight tumbled through the window to bronze him.

"I'm not defending them." She took a step back to really look at the man. What an arresting sight. Not that what she felt was attraction—she could not imagine. Her and Gage? But a woman could appreciate the pleasant look of a man, couldn't she? He was like a sculpture, a work of artistry, and his goodness shone through even his stormiest scowl.

"I'm just saying I know it's hard for you to be trapped with a bunch of single women in close quarters," she soothed. "Try and see below the surface. Maybe some of them have been hurt the same way you have."

"Then why are they so eager to hook themselves a husband?"

"Because they made the choice not to let one bad experience ruin their hope to find what matters most in life. Love."

"I knew you were going to say something corny like that." He rolled his eyes, but he didn't come across as harsh, nor as bristly. He strolled through an archway into a dark living room, and opened another shade. "They should figure out one of the most important facts of life. Love doesn't last. It's not worth chasing after."

"Real love lasts. Nothing could be more important." Matthew squealed, wanting to add his two-cents' worth to the conversation. She carried him through the dining room toward his uncle. "If love ends, then that's how you know it wasn't the real thing."

"Speaking from personal experience?"

"You know I am." It hurt. If only there was a way to stop it. But she wouldn't, even if she could. "At my grandmother's funeral, the minister said that grief is the price of love."

"One way or another, I suppose that's true. It's a price we've both paid by loving the wrong person."

"That's exactly what I did." Chalk it up to another failure in her life. Her parents had always been quick to point out her flaws—she was too short, her laugh was too loud, her job too blue-collar—but they had adored Alan. Losing him was not a failure, she told herself firmly. Not this time. It was the best thing that could have happened to her. Perhaps now she had the chance for a better life and greater happiness. "Could you imagine if he had bucked up his courage, kept his doubts silent and married me anyway?"

"It might have worked. The poor man must have loved you. How could someone not?"

His words touched her, and when she met his gaze, the sun became brighter, the sky bluer, the day extraordinary.

"Do you know what you just did?" she asked.

"Yes, and don't even say it." He might be grumbling, but not even Mr. Grinch himself could hide his true colors. "We aren't."

"We are," she insisted.

"No," he denied.

"We truly are friends now." She wanted to sing with delight. A total victory. "There's no going back. You can't undo this moment."

"Not even if I paid you to?" Humor darkened the mesmerizing blue of his eyes and softened the hard planes of his granite face. No man—ever—could be as magnificent as Gage as he tried not to laugh.

"Not even then," she assured him. "There isn't enough money on this planet."

"I don't know why you're bothering." He crossed behind a cabbage rose–patterned couch and opened another blind. "It's not as if you are going to be here long. Bucky is going to propose in another week and you'll be off planning your next wedding."

"Is that what you think?"

"Yes, and I don't think you will listen to a word of advice. I can stand here and warn you not to marry Bucky, and it will do no good. You're convinced love is a calm river with a few minor rapids that anyone can negotiate safely."

"I don't think there is anything safe about love." She adjusted Matthew on her hip, careful to hide the heart-break she carried within. "It's always a great risk."

"If only it came with a warning label. Then at least I would have been prepared. Love should *mean* something. Everything," he corrected. He opened the last window and stood in the frame of light. Silhouetted, she could not read his face, but she could feel his truth like summer's warmth on the wind.

The mystery of Gage Parker revealed.

"I get what you're saying about some of these women being more than what I see on the surface," he said. "I wish I could understand what it would take to trust again. I can't imagine ever wanting to."

"You thought the worst of me when we first met, remember?"

"Hard to forget the sight of you in a wedding gown kicking that tire."

"Not a moment I'm proud of."

They chuckled together and it was nice, a moment between friends.

She circled around an overstuffed chair to join Gage at the window. What a peaceful view, full of green trees, rugged mountains and sky. She leaned against the arm of the couch, ignoring the dust rising like chalk into the air. Matthew gave another shout and held out his little hands toward Gage. He fastened his big blue eyes on his uncle and began to babble excitedly.

"What's with him?" Gage studied the boy as if he were a strange alien being.

"I think he wants you to hold him."

"No, that can't be it. Maybe he needs his supper. We'd better head back to the house."

"Why Gage Parker, are you afraid of this baby?"

"I'm not afraid."

"Then why don't you take him? He wants you to."

"No, I'm sure he doesn't. I'm paying *you* to haul him around."

Oh, she had seen this before. One of her brothers-in-law had no experience with babies, and when her sister's daughter was born—the first infant in the family—Dirk did everything to avoid the fragile little one.

"I'm so not fooled." She held Matthew out to him. "Go on, take him. You won't drop him."

"I could."

"Impossible. It just feels that way at first, but you'll get used to it." She angled the boy toward Gage's strong shoulder—not that she ought to be noticing how wide and dependable his shoulders were. When Gage's arms wrapped around the baby, she adjusted his hand and the curve of his elbow to support the Matthew's weight. "See?"

"Take him back."

"Look how happy he is. He needs you, Gage."

"Ryan shouldn't have left him." He gazed down at the little guy and cleared emotion from his throat. "There was a staff meeting at work this morning, and my brother should have been there. Amy said she called his cell and left a message, but he never got back to her."

"So your brother is a tour guide, too?"

"Was, before he was laid off. Business is back up, and he ought to be in town ready to work and support his son. But instead of being responsible, he's off doing God knows what." Giving in to the anger was safer than feeling the painful disappointment. He thought of the argument they'd had a few weeks after Matthew was born. They'd never been able to patch things up since, and he regretted it. "Ryan is his own kind of drama."

"What kind of man is he?"

"That's just it. He's a man, but he's acting like a kid.

He fell in with a bad crowd after I left for college. Gran did what she could. I tried to help when I could, but I was busy and working two jobs to pay my way."

"That doesn't leave a lot of time for anything. I know. I've been there." She had taken an extra two years to get her degree juggling school and work. "Jean told me that Ryan never married Matthew's mother."

"They were engaged. I had him almost turned around, I think. I got him understanding he had to grow up. His fiancée, Wendy, had turned to Reverend Michaels for counsel. She got Ryan back in church, and I had hoped—" Gage's jaw tightened, and the tendons stood out in his neck.

"That he would finally step up to his responsibilities." Karenna finished the thought for him.

"And quit his partying ways for good. I failed him."

"Don't think that for a moment. I know you."

"You've practically just met me." The little guy's weight was warm and alive, but who captured all of his attention? Karenna. Her understanding fell across him like a new dawn. Hope, the first seeds of it, tried to bury deep in his soul.

"But sometimes you simply know someone," she said, simply. "You can see them more deeply."

"You'd better take him." He handed the baby back, and the boy protested with an indignant shout. "Sorry, Matthew. I've got a lot of work to do."

"What about supper?" She cuddled the boy against her.

"Keep a plate warm for me, would you?" He wanted distance from her. He felt revealed. She had a one-way ticket straight past his defenses, and he didn't like it. "I want to get some work done out here."

"All right." She studied him for a moment. He prayed she didn't guess his feelings—and she must not have, because she retreated with Matthew in her arms. "We'll leave you in peace."

He doubted that. Peace would not be possible as long as that woman was within a hundred yards of him.

She left, and the shadows within him deepened. He could no longer hide from the truth.

Karenna set the fragrant bowl of garlic mashed potatoes on the table and surveyed her work. The roast looked juicy and savory, the green beans buttery and steaming and the gravy thick and flavorful. Warm rolls gave off a yeasty scent from the basket at Gage's elbow. Satisfaction filled her. Her work was done. She wasn't technically a chef, but she liked kitchen work; and Jean looked less fragile with less work to do, so it seemed like the perfect reason to insist on making dinner. Now it was time for her to go.

"Enjoy." She knelt to kiss Matthew's cheek.

"Eee!" He smacked his palm on his high chair tray and flashed his dimples.

"Good night, Karenna." Jean beamed from her chair, looking as if a burden was off her shoulders. "I can't thank you enough."

"It was my pleasure. I intend to make fixing meals for you all a habit." She could feel Gage's piercing gaze— surely he had recovered from their awkward moment last night. *Please don't let him think I'm trying to show off my wifely skills,* she prayed, as she grabbed her purse and headed for the door. "My car is ready, so I've got to get on the road."

"On your bicycle?" Gage arched one brow drolly, and

it was hard to tell if he was amused by her bicycling or disapproving.

That man. He did affect her more than she wanted him to. So if her heart skipped a beat, she firmly denied it as she headed outside. The screen door whispered shut, cutting off the deep, serious sound of his voice as he began the blessing.

All in all, things went better with Gage today. At least it hadn't been as uncomfortable as that moment on the Michaelses' porch. She wheeled her borrowed bike away from the porch rails and swung onto the seat. Pedaling down the driveway, beneath the sun-dappled evergreen boughs and a perfect blue sky, made her feel as if everything was going to work out just right. She had to believe that God had brought her here for a higher purpose, and she was determined to make the most of this opportunity He had given her.

Chapter Eight

Head pounding—he did not have a good night of sleep—Gage leaned forward in his deck chair and hazarded a glance down the driveway, braced for another encounter with Karenna. When her familiar purple sports car rolled toward him, he took a steadying breath and braced himself. He spotted Karenna's mane of golden blond curls and her amazing smile behind the glare of the windshield.

Remember, you don't like her, he told himself. So what if she was the most gorgeous woman alive? If the images of her last night in his kitchen remained plastered to the inside of his brain? He didn't want to care. He wasn't interested in her.

Sure, and maybe if he said that enough times he might talk himself into it.

She pulled in next to the garage. Her window was down, giving him a perfect view of her, morning fresh and lovely in a light turquoise blouse. When she climbed from the car, it was hard not to notice the fashionable short pants she wore, the kind that showed off her slender calves and the matching sandals on her feet.

"You look awfully chipper this morning," she said, in greeting. "Less like a bear, more like a man."

"No tours for me today."

"Then what will you do with your time?"

"Pester you?"

"Just try it." She kept going into the light until the sunshine enveloped her and it was too bright looking into the sun to see her.

"You must be glad to have your car back," he observed.

"Bucky was incredible. I can't believe he got a new radiator installed so fast."

There we go, Gage thought, *back to Bucky.*

"I mean, no offense, but Treasure Creek is out in the boonies. Probably not in Alaskan terms, but definitely in mine. I'm ecstatic he could get my car fixed. I have wheels again." Her footsteps padded on the wooden stairs, and she rose up out of the blinding rays like a blessing. "And it runs better than ever."

"Bucky's a good mechanic, sure." Gage's teeth ground together. Easy to imagine the younger fellow putting on the charm for Karenna *and* moving her car to the top of his repair list.

Not that he was in competition with the man. Why did his jaw stay clamped as tight as a vise? His teeth ached. He couldn't seem to unclamp them. "Suppose you and he—"

"What? Oh, not you, too." She rolled her eyes with a huff. "No, we're not dating."

"The only question is, when's the wedding? I need as much notice as you can give me. It's tough finding a good nanny." Not only his teeth were hurting, but now pain radiated down his jawbone. A bad sign—of what, he was afraid to ponder.

"I'm not going to marry Bucky," she insisted.

"Why not? You already have a dress."

"Ruined beyond saving, I expect." She padded backward toward the house. The long, low rays of sunshine seemed to fall at her feet, surrounding her with a wholesome glow that made his heart come back to life. Unaware, she settled her backpack higher on her shoulder. "How about I whip up a batch of whole wheat blueberry pancakes and sizzle up some turkey bacon?"

"That sounds pretty healthy. I don't approve of healthy."

"Why am I not surprised? I'm not sure if you approve of much, Mountain Man. Get off your duff and come help me."

"Didn't I say this was my day off?"

"I heard you." Amusement lifted the notes of her voice as she tugged open the screen door. "This is your chance to make good on your word."

"What word?"

"That you can cook." She padded into the relative dimness of the kitchen, lost from his sight, but not from his senses.

His ears strained to hear the cadence of her shoes on the linoleum, his eyes searched the shadows for any glimpse of her. His presence sought hers with a force he could not stop.

Maybe this is friendship I'm feeling. He took a final swig of coffee from his cup, planted his feet on the deck and stood. *Yep, that's what this is, friendship*—not anything frightening, and nothing that would demand more of him than he could risk losing.

"Put me to work," he said, slamming his mug down on the counter.

"Excellent." She whirled from the refrigerator with the milk carton in hand. "Wash up."

"Already on it." He turned on the faucet and soaped up. "What's on your agenda for today?"

"No real plans." She added eggs and a carton of blueberries to the counter and searched through the pantry for a bag of pancake mix. "Why?"

"I was hoping you would help me with the garage apartment."

"That place definitely needs some help." She searched through a drawer for measuring cups and a spoon. "Count me in."

"I appreciate it. It's a big job, and with two of us it will go quicker." He grabbed the blueberry carton and began rinsing the berries in the sink. "What did you think of the place?"

"It's cozy, and it could be really cute if it's painted." She measured milk into the bowl. "I'm sure if you put a note on the bulletin board at church you could get it rented in a nanosecond."

"I wanted to fix it up for you. You should live here."

"Me?" Shock pounded through her. She set down the milk carton before she dropped it. "Are you serious?"

"Aren't I always?" Dimples crept into the corners of his smile.

Gage Parker had dimples. Who knew?

"I would love to live here. Now I can't *wait* to get started cleaning the place. Hurry up." She speared the wooden spoon into the bowl and began mixing. This had to be a sign from above. She'd been without direction, and then she found the magazine article. She'd come here without a job and found one. Now she would have a place to live. It was as if heaven were clearing her path, but where was God leading her?

Just trust, she told herself, as Gage chuckled.

"The berries are clean. I hear Matthew. No, let me. You keep cooking. I'm going to try my newly acquired expertise with the boy."

"You mean the skill of being able to hold him?"

"Hey, it's a start." Gage flashed a full-on smile, one that warmed his midnight blue eyes.

Thunk went her heart, falling in one long tumble.

I'm in big trouble, she thought, reaching for the blueberries. *Big, big trouble.*

She was a hard worker, and he should know, since he'd hardly been able to take his attention from her all morning. He gave the armoire a few more shoves and it stubbornly creaked a few more inches along the decades-old carpet before grating to a stop.

"Need help?" Karenna straightened from the vacuum with a full bag of lint. A single line of dust streaked her forehead. She looked adorable.

"No, I got it." Sure, the armoire was heavy, but that wasn't the reason he was having trouble with it. He focused his attention on his work, swiped his damp brow and put his shoulder into it. His muscles strained and the heavy piece of furniture began to slide. "If I get the furniture in the middle of the room and tarped, we can think about painting."

"Especially since the place is dust free." Karenna dumped the bag in the garbage can on the deck. "This isn't exactly a fun way for you to spend your day off."

"I don't mind, and the company isn't so bad."

She rewarded with him a smile that made the day brighter. The aching muscles in his back were forgotten.

It was true, he realized, as he eased the piece of furniture into place with the others, and, done, gave a prayer of thanks. Karenna's help today had been a blessing—and not because of the work she'd done. She had made a morning of drudgery enjoyable.

"See? This friendship thing is good." She returned to the vacuum and wound up the cord. "Admit it. I was right."

"I wouldn't go that far." He said, grousing, but he felt like laughing. "I'd say our friendship is survivable."

"You are the most cynical man I've ever met."

"Thank you. I sure try hard. It's good to know my efforts have paid off."

She laughed, a merry sound that made him happier just to listen to it. She shoved the vacuum across the floor and out onto the deck. "Do you know what color would look perfect in here?"

"Don't say it. Not one word. I'm painting these walls white. End of discussion."

"I would believe you, except for that twinkle in your eye."

"There's no twinkle. I don't allow twinkles. I don't approve of them." He drew himself up full height, as if he were ready to lay down the law, but it was only to make her laugh again.

"Light yellow." She apparently wasn't daunted by him. "It's perfect for the exposure and for the woodwork."

"White." He grabbed one of the water bottles on the counter and upended it. This friendship thing wasn't bad—not at all. Fact was, he enjoyed it.

"How about I pick a pale yellow shade that's almost white?"

"Done." The bottle was empty, so he tossed it into

the bag set aside for recyclables. "After lunch, want to head into town? I can buy paint at the General Store."

"Deal." She gathered the mop and bucket full of cleaning supplies from the main house and carried them out the door. "How long do you think it will take to paint?"

"We can be done by tomorrow. Give it a day to dry and you can move in Sunday night or Monday morning."

"Excellent." She thought of her things packed up and in storage back in Seattle. Originally, she would have had her things moved to Alan's condo after the honeymoon, but now she would have them shipped. She intended to stay in Alaska and make a life here in Treasure Creek.

The sun was high in the sky, bearing down with bone-warming summer's heat. The lazy breeze stirred the trees and carried a chickadee's song, and she did her best to lug the mop and bucket without dropping anything. Difficult, because her attention was on the man scooping up the vacuum and following her down the stairs.

So far so good, she told herself. Her heart may have taken a dive, but she had managed to keep it from showing. She led the way onto the backyard, where Matthew sat in the shade on a blanket, playing with a half-dozen plastic cups. He beat them together like cymbals, adding his own musical squeals.

"He's giving a concert." Jean straightened from weeding her vegetable garden. "Let's hope he never wants a set of drums."

"He might want to accompany the church choir one day." Karenna couldn't resist teasing. Happiness bubbled through her, leaving her buoyant. She wasn't sure her feet fully touched the ground as she strolled across the lawn. "Jean, you shouldn't be doing that work, or at least not alone. It's too much."

"I'm seventy-five. That's still young in my book!" Indomitable, Jean climbed to her feet and peeled off her pink work gloves. "Besides, nothing is going to make me give up my gardening. Did you kids get the apartment in shape?"

"Almost." She stopped when Matthew dropped his cups, held out his hands and squealed in glee. Not at her, she realized, but at the big man ambling behind her. "I think he wants you, Gage."

"Me? I'm busy." That gruff bark didn't fool her one bit.

"Go on, make him happy. Pick him up."

"He's fine right where he is." His excuse didn't fool her, either.

"Don't worry, Matthew." She unloaded her bucket and mop on the deck and yanked the vacuum out of Gage's hands. "Your uncle adores you. It's hard for him to show his feelings."

Matthew squealed as if in answer, hands held out, begging to be picked up.

"You're in demand." She dared to lay a hand on Gage's forearm. He was sun-warmed iron. His gaze raked hers and she wasn't sure if she read gratitude there or something deeper.

The baby called out again, his big baby-blues focused on his uncle with poignant need. Matthew's feet kicked, his entire body trembling with his enthusiasm.

"What's up with you, little man?" Gage's buttery baritone warmed.

Matthew preened for him, joyous that the object

of his affection was coming for him. He reached out, wobbling animatedly.

"Whoa, there." Gage's chuckle rumbled like low notes, musical and captivating. He knelt, caught the boy and scooped him into his arms. Matthew's coo of bliss brightened the sunlight. He giggled and snuggled against his uncle's broad chest. His fists clenched tightly to Gage's T-shirt.

The world faded away, the chirp and chatter of birdsong silenced until there was only Gage. The man who didn't let anyone close, who kept even family members at arm's length, stood as rigid as a marble statue. His every muscle tensed, his jaw became a harsh, clenched line as he wrestled to keep the guards up, and then struggled to let them down.

His jaw softened, his muscles relaxed and he nestled his cheek against Matthew's downy head.

I'm in such trouble, she thought, falling a little bit farther for him.

Trouble didn't even begin to describe it.

Matthew's cheerful squeals from the backseat accompanied them on their way to town. Gage glanced more than a few times in the rearview to catch a glimpse of the little fellow. He looked as pleased as punch, beating a plastic block against his car seat. Affection, more than what was safe, wrapped like a ribbon around his ribs. There was no point in denying it. It was too late to stop it. *Now* what was he going to do?

Karenna, in the front passenger seat, inches away, was the cause. His defenses had been up, and he'd made his mind up not to like her. Not anymore.

So much for best-laid plans. He caught sight of the Welcome To Treasure Creek sign on the outskirts of town and eased off the gas for the reduced speed limit.

"Matthew seems a lot happier since you started holding him. Look at him. He's babbled nonstop since you buckled him into his car seat." She seemed honest and true, with her sincere blue eyes trained on him.

Be careful, he warned himself, *or you might start believing in her.*

"It's not because of me. Matthew got too much fresh air." He put on his best frown. He didn't know what was wrong—he couldn't remember frowning once since they'd gotten into the Jeep together.

"You're wrong. Matthew has good taste," she said, correcting him, stubbornly cheerful.

He was beginning to see that Karenna was stubbornly cheerful about everything.

"Taste? What taste. Matthew is currently sucking on a blue block." He stopped for a flock of pedestrians crossing the road. The women in designer garb and the latest fashions looked like tropical birds against the rugged backdrop of wild mountains and rustic town.

"Admit it, Gage. You liked holding him."

"Is it your job to give me a hard time?"

"No, but it is a perk."

"That reminds me. I'm your boss. An employer shouldn't have to put up with this." Town was no longer the sane, quiet place he'd come to love. Everywhere he looked, cars took up all the on-street parking, idled in the street while pedestrians crossed, or waited for parking spaces.

Change. He didn't like it. He didn't approve of it, and it was happening all around him. Worse, he feared, it was happening to *him,* and he knew just who to blame.

The woman sitting next to him with the girl-next-door charm.

"An employer, no," she agreed. "But you and I aren't merely boss and worker bee. We are also—"

"Don't say it," he ground out, as if he were in a temper. The trouble was, his bitterness was nowhere in sight. He wasn't happy about that—not at all.

"Friends." She uttered the one word he could no longer deny. Mischief animated her. How could she look cuter every time he looked at her? "The dictionary defines friends as being attached by esteem, someone who is not hostile, a kindly companion. I looked it up."

"Smarty." He told himself he wasn't amused. And since he wasn't charmed by her, either, he ought to keep the glare on his face and the glower to his personality.

If only he could.

"I know what you're doing."

"I don't know what you're talking about," she denied, as if she couldn't possibly be culpable.

He spotted brake lights and stopped, hitting his turn signal. Someone was leaving a parking space almost directly in front of Harry's place. The General Store looked packed. He hazarded a sidelong glance at Karenna, who strained against her seat belt to get a look up and down the sidewalk, taking it all in.

When he spoke, he heard the warmth in his voice and hated that it showed. "You are worming your way into our lives, Gran's, Matthew's and mine, with this friendship thing."

"Can you blame me?" She faced him, her golden curls bouncing, her force of life so awesome he momentarily lost the ability to parallel park and the front tire hit the curb. She seemed unaware of her affect on him. "You are good people, Gage. Some of the best I've met."

"Now you're exaggerating, if you are including me in that." He jockeyed the SUV into position.

"I most certainly am not exaggerating. I've gotten a good glimpse of the bearish side of your personality, remember the night we met?" She unbuckled her seat belt. "I think I've seen enough of the real you to know what I'm talking about."

"Ditto." He withdrew his keys from the ignition. "When I first saw you, I made an assumption, too."

"That I was a flake in a wedding dress? That I was a woman looking for a wedding ring and a man's paycheck?"

"You showed me how disillusioned I've become. You're all right, Karenna."

"Coming from you, that's high praise."

"Bingo." He cracked a smile. "How about we get the painting supplies? I can tell you're itching to get that apartment ready."

"I am. I'm going to make the place so cute you won't recognize it. I might never want to leave."

"So you've made up your mind to stay in Treasure Creek?"

"I'm falling in love with this town." Heat stained her face.

Thank heavens Gage didn't think twice about her choice of words or her enthusiasm. His door swung open, letting in a whiff of breeze. As he circled around the front of the Jeep, she bent to grab Matthew's diaper bag off the floor at her feet, hoping that her blush would go away. Why did she feel so transparent, as if her ever-burgeoning regard for Gage was visible for all to see?

Gage got her door and took her hand in his much

larger one. His fingers enclosed hers. As he helped her from the seat, she felt airborne and weightless, as if the world stopped spinning and God froze the moment. Everything within her stilled. Her affections dove deeper against her will.

Then her feet touched the sidewalk, people strolled by in a blur of color and conversation and Gage released his hold on her. The world went back to normal. Everything looked unchanged—except for her.

"C'mon, buddy." Gage gathered the baby from the backseat, holding him handily in one arm.

Matthew jabbered ecstatically, his dark hair and blue eyes so like his uncle's. They could be father and son, Karenna realized with a jolt.

Don't even go there, she ordered herself. Don't even think about what Gage's baby would look like. Not a little bit. She shook her head, trying to clear it, but she couldn't. Her thoughts were so busy she almost didn't hear her cell ring.

"Go ahead and get that." Gage handed over Matthew. "I'll get started on the list."

"Thanks." Adrenaline spiked through her as she settled Matthew on one hip. Her phone continued to jangle, and she was tempted to let it ring. She feared it was Maryann, calling her again to try and talk some sense into her, or failing that, to make good on her promise to come to Alaska.

Letting a call like that go to voicemail wasn't going to solve a thing. Might as well get it over with, she told herself. Dug her phone out of the outside compartment on the diaper bag and flipped it open. "Hello?"

Chapter Nine

"Karenna?"

A familiar man's voice filled her ear, echoing around in her foggy head. It took her a moment to recognize him. "Alan?"

"Yes, it's me, honey."

Her knees went weak. Shock pummeled her and she needed to sit down. She spotted a bench in front of a neighboring business and arrowed to it. The sidewalk was busy. She wove around a grizzled, muttering man, squeezed around two women dressed like fashion magazine models and tumbled breathlessly onto the empty bench.

"I know you're surprised to hear from me," he was saying. "I meant to call earlier, but you can imagine how hard it was for me to dial your number."

"No, I can't." She settled Matthew on her lap. He grabbed at the phone, talking elatedly.

Here it comes, she thought, and braced her back against the bench's wooden slats—planted her feet on the ground and readied herself for the wave of misery to strike. It didn't. "I can't believe what you did to me, Alan."

"What I did to you? I was simply being honest. Things were all happening too fast for me."

"We'd been together for seven years and engaged for two." Had Alan always used the words "I" and "me" so much?

"I got cold feet. I'm sorry. My mother is terribly disappointed in me," he went on. "I hear your mom refuses to speak to you."

"I'm busy, Alan." She felt a tingle on the back of her neck and twisted around, searching the unfamiliar faces of the people parading by on the sidewalk. She didn't recognize anyone. Then she saw him—Gage—watching her from the window. Their gazes locked and she felt a catch in her chest, like her heart kick-starting for the first time.

"Karenna?" A voice said in her ear. "Are you there?"

"Oh, right. Alan." She felt breathless when Gage lifted his hand in a single manly wave of acknowledgement. She sat powerless to move, held captive by the tug of the emotional bond between them. "Why exactly are you calling?"

"To ask you to take me back. Forget the letter I wrote. I was confused. I didn't mean it."

Gage moved away from the window out of the reach of her sight but not out of her feelings. He remained like the sun at the center of her world.

Lord, please help me, she prayed. *Please help me to stop falling any further for the man.*

"Karenna? I'm ready to marry you now." Alan broke into her thoughts. "I didn't realize how much I would miss you. It's a terrible ache. I can't stand it."

"Just an ache?" Funny, that's what he had been to her, too. She had thought she loved him, and she had, but she hadn't been experienced enough to know the companionship they'd shared lacked luster and a deep emotional connection. Now, because of Gage, she could see that love, when it was true, was more.

"You know what I mean. My life isn't the same without you."

"Even if I'm too much to deal with?" She used his exact phrase from his letter.

"See, there you go again. You know I have a problem with your temper. And you have to admit you can be stubborn, and you take charge of things and run with it. But none of that matters right now."

"Yes, it does." She had come close to marrying a man who didn't love her, at least not more than he loved himself. She could see that now, and gave great thanks that God had led her to Treasure Creek. In coming here, she had learned important things about herself—that she could stand on her own two feet and make a new start. And the window God had opened for her was just what her spirit had been searching for.

"Will you come home and marry me?" Alan asked, sounding sure of himself, as if he was such a great catch she would leap at the chance.

"No, I'm sorry." What had she ever seen in him?

"No? You're saying no to me?"

"I have to." She didn't love him now, and most important of all, he was not the man she wanted. He wasn't Gage. "Goodbye."

"Karenna, I—"

She flipped the phone shut. Matthew reached for it, a dear weight in her arms. She gently leaned her cheek against his soft head, held him close and let the breeze cool her face.

I've made a terrible mistake, she thought.

She had fallen in love with Gage and there was no going back.

* * *

Gage spotted the familiar face on his way toward the checkout counter in the jam-packed store. Although more than several weeks had passed since Tucker's father's funeral, he was surprised his old friend was still in town. He pushed his loaded cart into line. "Hey, buddy."

"Gage. It's good to see you, man."

"What are you up to?" He'd been meaning to get ahold of his old friend. "Looks like you're going fishing?"

"I'm heading out for a de-stress trip this evening." Tucker Lawson looked as if he needed it. The impeccable lawyer didn't seem himself. Dark circles and a haggard look hinted he hadn't been getting much sleep. "A friend is lending me his plane. I'm going to get away from it all. Get some mulling time. Try to find some peace."

"Grief is tough." Gage had been there over his own father long ago. "It can throw you for a loop. Change your perspective on things."

"It sure can. I also had a tough case, and it's weighing on my conscience." Tucker raked a hand through his hair, the troubled look deepening on his face.

"It sounds like this trip is just what you need. When you get back, we ought to get together."

"It's a deal." Tucker attempted a grin, but it didn't work.

Gage knew exactly what it was like to carry a burden. The weight of his bitterness remained, and it was beginning to get too heavy to carry around.

"Check out this woman," Tucker leaned in, keeping his voice low and nodding toward the middle-aged woman with big, bleached blond hair and a mountain of purchases. "I think she's trying to get old Harry's attention."

"I think she's trying to do more than that. She's going to sprain her eyelashes if she keeps batting them so fast." Gage put a hand on the boxed air-conditioning unit to keep it steady on the top of the cart. To think he'd once mistakenly assumed Karenna was desperate like that.

"How much longer do we have to wait, Harry?" Tucker called out to the slightly grumpy store owner who was totaling up what looked like a good quarter of the store.

"Hold on a minute, Jolene." Harry swiped a strand of salt-and-pepper hair from his eyes and tossed a pad and two pencils down the counter. "You boys write down what you got there and I'll bill you later. Don't forget, I've known you both since you were in diapers, so be honest."

"Looks like you've got your hands full." Gage caught a pencil.

Harry didn't comment. Apparently, it took all of a man's concentration to avoid giving in to a lady's ardent attentions.

Gage knew how that felt, too. He glanced over his shoulder, but he wasn't standing where he could see the bench from the window. Karenna had looked down when she'd been on the phone. Who had called her and why? Panic erupted inside him at the possibilities. Could be her mother begging Karenna to come home. Or one of her sisters reminding her of the life she'd left behind. Or maybe it was the runaway groom himself, wanting a second chance with her.

Face it, Gage, she is going to leave one day, one way or another. He had to accept it. As much as he cared for her, she would wind up leaving him. Maybe not today, but an opportunity would come for her—another job, another man, another marriage proposal—and he would have to let her go.

He hardened his heart so he wouldn't feel the blow of pain. He was already attached to her. He had let her too far in, and he didn't have a clue what to do about it. He bent to his work, scribbling down the paint, brushes and pans on the small tablet, and bagging his own purchases.

After wishing Tucker a good trip, he ran into another good friend on the way to the door. Jake Rodgers looked up, a spool of fishing line in hand. "Hey, buddy. Is that your new nanny outside?"

"Word travels fast, huh?" He knew how rumors flew with lightning speed in a small town, so why was he blushing? Doing his best to act casual, he gave an indifferent shrug. "Had to hire someone. The only good thing about all these women in town is that I could finally find someone to take care of Matthew."

"For a minute, I was hoping you might get other ideas."

Jake was a bachelor, too. Maybe he understood how lonely it was.

But that didn't mean he had to risk having his heart battered again. Could he help it that his gaze wandered toward the window? The sight of Karenna sitting on the bench was like an assurance to his soul.

"The chief's looking for you." Jake chuckled, as if he'd just figured out the punch line to a good joke. "Something about the last search-and-rescue you did. The hikers wound up lost on my land."

"There's always paperwork." Gage tried to look disgruntled, but in truth, he couldn't focus. Karenna kept taking over his thoughts. He liked how she sat so poised on the wooden bench, looking as if she belonged there, bronzed by sunlight and framed by the rugged mountains rising up just out of town. What were the chances she really might stay like she said? He dismissed it even as he thought it. "Guess I'd best go find Reed. Get things straightened out while I'm in town."

"See you, Gage." Jake looked like he was trying to hold back a chuckle. "Glad you found someone. For Matthew, that is."

"Me, too. What do I know about babies?" He managed to stay in denial as he headed toward the door and made his way outside. But it began to waver when she turned toward him, as if she were able to sense his presence.

No one on this planet could be as lovely as Karenna Digby. She fastened her sad gaze on him, and as she drew herself up straight, he saw a hint of strength in her that he'd never guessed at. Strength and dignity and courage. It made him wonder about her phone call.

"Looks as if you found everything." She shifted Matthew on her lap and went to pocket her phone. She didn't seem ready to talk about it.

"No, stay where you are. There's no reason you and the boy shouldn't enjoy the scenery a bit more." He wove around a group of women. She was his focus, his center. "I've got to run a few doors down and see the police chief for a few minutes. Do you mind?"

"Not at all. Matthew and I are having fun watching everyone go by. And this way, I can keep trying to get ahold of my cousin."

"Is something wrong?" Maybe that was what the call was about. A family problem of some sort. He didn't want to analyze the relief sweeping through him. He wanted her former groom to stay far away.

"I can't seem to get a hold of her, which is really odd." Karenna's sadness was background, something she was struggling to hide. "She's left a few brief messages. I don't know why. Probably because she said she was going to save me from myself."

"Lord knows you need help, Karenna."

"I've heard that before." Her chuckle rang light and easy, but it didn't last. Sure enough, something was troubling her. "You would like Maryann. She has an attitude of doom about marriage, too. She is very concerned I'm going to up and marry the first available Alaskan bachelor I come across."

"She sounds very sensible to me." He winked, for some reason, he wasn't able to get into his marriage-is-doom point of view. He opened the back of the Jeep and laid the packages inside. "I won't be more than a few minutes."

"Perfect."

Why did his feet seem to drag as he forced them away from her? He didn't want to know the answer. He gritted his teeth and stalked down the sidewalk. The women new to town were like an obstacle course. They stopped suddenly to peer into windows or exclaim over a moose wandering down an alley. He had to avoid crashing into their shopping bags. He had to circle around huddles of ladies exchanging pleasantries. Then he spotted someone familiar up ahead. He lengthened his stride to catch up with the young mother and her two little boys.

"Amy." He loped up beside her.

"Gage." She brightened when she saw him. Her sons, ages three and four, were as cute as could be. They both beamed up at him. "Hi, Uncle Gage."

"Howdy, boys." He knew Amy well enough to be

able to recognize the tension tight in her jaw. She looked worried, although she was trying to hide it.

Sympathy filled him up. She was a young mother on her own, raising two boys and trying to keep her company afloat. She had a lot of responsibility. "What brings you to town?" he asked.

"I've got to see Reed." Her jaw snapped shut, betraying her tension.

"Reed?" Her reason really had to be an important one. Anyone close to Amy knew of Reed Truscott's well-intentioned marriage proposal after Ben's death. Of course, Amy hadn't wanted a convenient marriage, and she'd held it against the man ever since. "Tell me what's wrong."

"Not here." Only then did he notice her hand on her purse clasp, as if to protect something inside.

Interesting. He opened the door for her and the boys, glancing up the street. Karenna drew him like gravity, and he didn't even try to resist, but he couldn't spot her. A group of women window shopping obstructed his view.

Cool air drifted over him, reminding him where he was. He shook thoughts of Karenna out of his head and followed Amy into the air-conditioned office. The little kids dashed inside, their shoes beating against the tile, their voices high with excitement at seeing Reed. The boys were chattering on about how they had their very own map and they were treasure hunters. Did Reed want to be one, too?

"What's all this?" Reed scooped Sammy onto his desk and then did the same with Dexter. "Have you boys have been playing prospector again?"

"It's the legend." Instead of looking amused, Amy

continued to look a bit tense and worried. "Maybe you ought to take care of Gage first."

"No," Gage spoke up. "Ladies first. Besides, I'm curious. Is it something I can help with?"

"You're a good friend. Ben and I were always able to count on you." Amy nodded once, as if making a decision, and opened her purse. "But I need this to stay quiet. Between the three of us."

"Sure." Gage shrugged, exchanging looks with Reed. Reed had a protective glint in his eyes, and judging by the hard set of his face, the man had already figured Amy had some kind of trouble and was serious about helping her.

Good. No one would be better for Amy than Reed.

"It's the legend." She withdrew a plastic storage bag from her purse. Inside was a thick roll of paper. "I think it's real."

"What's real?" Reed asked, opening his desk drawer to hand two small lollipops—both red—to each boy.

"Two little cookie hunters were digging around in my kitchen cabinets and look what they found in a hidden compartment in the wall." She withdrew the map from the protective bag and handed it to him.

Gage's stomach cinched. Could it be her great-great-grandfather's treasure map?

"I checked the handwriting in the family Bible," Amy explained. "It matches Mack Tanner's exactly."

"Let me take a look." Reed took it from her. Time stood still as he studied the fragile parchment, the precise instructions and the marked trail that led to what was rumored to be a fortune. He brushed one fingertip across the red X. "I think your boys did it, Amy. This must be the real thing."

"Let me see." Gage shouldered over, taking in the

aged paper and the old-fashioned handwriting. "It looks authentic to me."

"Me, too." She carefully spooled the parchment into a tidy roll. "That's why I brought it here to you, Reed. Now I'm trusting you both with the information. This was an untold fortune in 1898. Think what it would be worth now."

"No. Don't think it." A muscle snapped in Reed's jaw. "Best that you put this map back and forget you found it."

"But—"

"Don't you see? Folks get wind of this, especially all these new people in town. A bunch of crazy treasure hunts isn't an answer to your problems. The city's search-and-rescue costs alone would skyrocket."

"Sounds sensible to me," Gage agreed. Although he figured that wasn't the answer Amy wanted to hear.

"But think of the money, Reed," she said.

"I am. Financially, we can't handle the demand we've already got. Add to that people getting hurt or lost chasing after gold. Those mountains are dangerous. That would be just the start of the trouble."

Gage added his two cents' worth. "That's a fact. Think of the trouble we have now with all these city folk wandering around and getting lost. Nothing bad has happened yet, but if we add modern-day gold fever to the mix, who can tell what trouble there might be?"

"Yes, I know." Amy agreed. She gingerly tucked the map into her purse. "But not if no one else knows about it. This is just between us."

"It wouldn't work." Reed stood firm, and Gage agreed with him. "You know what they say about a small town? Nothing stays secret for long. Word of this gets around, and folks will get pesky. Others might get dangerous. They could come after you. No, Amy, I wouldn't risk it."

"That's not the reaction I expected. This merits a little more thought." She glanced toward the window. "Thanks for being honest with me, both of you. I'll consider what you've advised."

"Good. You have any trouble, you'll call me?" Reed's dark gaze searched hers. He was concerned for her. There was no missing it.

Gage wondered when Amy was going to figure out Reed truly cared for her.

"There isn't going to be any trouble." She marched straight to the boys. Soon they were all pounding through the office to the front door, lollipops in hand. "No one knows about the map, unless you tell."

"My lips are sealed," Gage spoke up.

"Things have a way of coming out." Reed seemed sure of his prediction, which didn't have a good effect on Amy. She looked slightly annoyed at him. She kept her chin up and did not take a second look back as she headed for the door. "Goodbye, Reed. Gage, I'll see you Monday morning bright and early."

She ushered her little boys out the door, both talking cheerfully about wanting to hunt for buried treasure, and the door swung shut behind them. They made a nice picture, walking along the sidewalk and out of sight, a woman and her children. He wondered if Reed thought so, too, and if he was hoping to add himself to that picture.

"Word is going to get out, just you wait," Reed predicted, moving to his desk. "Now, I'm glad you dropped by. Let me find the report. I saw you drive by earlier with a pretty lady in your Jeep."

"Don't even start." Gage rolled his eyes, gritted his teeth and did his best to keep images of Karenna from filling his mind and, worse, his heart.

Chapter Ten

Gage was unusually quiet on the way home, which was fine with Karenna. They had stopped by the market for dinner—she thought a big pot of spaghetti and meatballs would hit the spot tonight and be something easy for Jean to heat up over the weekend. She was unusually quiet, too. She kept going over and over what she had realized after Alan's call.

I'm in love with Gage. This wasn't a harmless crush or a simple friendship. This was more than friendship, and at a heightened level, something she had never felt before. It was a power that wrapped around her, capturing her every vulnerability, and would not let her go.

What would Gage think if he knew? She risked a glance in his direction as the SUV bounced into the driveway. He drove the way he did everything, with purpose, capability and focus.

"I picked up some new fuses." He didn't seem aware of her heightened interest or that her affections had changed. "The garage is old. Wired before the standard breaker boxes."

"How come the garage is older than the house?"

"Because I had the place built when I moved back to Treasure Creek. I got the property for a bargain. The original house had burned down."

"Electrical problems?"

"How did you guess? Don't worry about the apartment. It was inspected when I bought the place. I've got an electrician coming as soon as he can work it into his schedule. In the meantime, I'll go over the wiring as much as I can. My real concern is that the air-conditioning unit might blow a fuse. Run it only if you need it."

She thought of the extras Gage had purchased for the apartment. The AC unit was a luxury, something thoughtful—but she had caught glimpses of other things in the bags when he'd loaded up his purchases—a smoke detector, a new coffeepot, a few light fixtures, several fans and new window blinds.

The SUV rounded a corner and the house—and Jean—came into sight.

"What is she doing?" Karenna zeroed in on the older woman kneeling before the front yard flower beds.

"Exactly what you told her not to do." Gage sounded amused.

"I said I would help her with that. It's a lot of work."

"Hey, don't look at me. I was going to take care of the weeds when I mowed."

"She's your grandmother. You need to make her take it easy."

"Karenna, I know what you're doing." He glanced sideways at her, his mood light, his dimples cutting into his lean face. "I'm no fool."

"No, I've never thought you were. What am I doing?"

"You don't know? Or are you denying it?"

"Denying what?" She looked puzzled.

"Don't think I haven't noticed. You have taken over the cooking, so Gran doesn't feel she needs to fuss with it." He pulled into the shade of the garage and cut the engine. "You've improved the quality of her meals, out of consideration for her diabetes."

"I worry about her." Not the whole truth, because her face belied her words. Judging by the way she warmed, she did a great deal more than simply worry about Gran. Karenna truly cared for the older woman.

"I'm paying you to be Matthew's nanny, not to cook and clean and take over the household errands." He climbed out of the SUV and popped open the back, but could he coerce his gaze away from Karenna?

No. She held him with a magnetic force, and he was helpless to resist.

"I'm aware of that," she said, as she flung open her door and leaped to the ground before he could reach her. There was something different about her, something he couldn't put his finger on as she opened the back door to fetch Matthew out of his seat. "This little one is a delight to care for, so I feel as if I needed to do more to earn my pay."

"I don't believe you."

"Why not?"

"Because I think that's only part of the story." He hefted the grocery bags, leaving the rest of the purchases for later. As he followed her into the dappled sunlight falling between the tall stands of trees, he kept trying to figure out why she looked different. Not sad, although he suspected that phone call in town, the one she avoided mentioning, had definitely made her sad. But that wasn't it.

"When you first came," he confessed, "I couldn't believe anyone would be so altruistic."

"You were very suspicious of me. I notice you aren't now."

"No." He'd never seen a more sincere woman; and the way she seemed to float along, as if she were following some inner song, became dear to him, like so many other things about her—things he was afraid to list. Not only would the tally be overwhelming, but it might point out what he was avoiding most. "I appreciate the way you've barged in and taken over."

"Wait. When you use words like 'barged in' and 'taken over', it doesn't sound like a compliment." She kept her tone light, walking away from him with sleeping Matthew in her arms, but he sensed something more.

"What did I do?" He'd bungled again, saying the wrong thing, missing some clue he should have noticed. "I've made you sad."

"No, not even close." She set her chin, a determined gesture, but he could read the pinch around her soft mouth that told a different story.

"I thought we were friends." He decided to use their relationship to get to the deeper truth. "Aren't friends supposed to share?"

"I see what you're up to, Gage Parker." She padded up the deck steps with a jaunty gait. He could feel the shadows trailing her. "It's nothing you want to hear about."

"Try me." The grocery sacks crinkled and rustled as he grabbed the screen door for her. "I've been going through a personal growth period. I might surprise you."

"You don't want to talk about Alan." She breezed into

the kitchen, a force to be reckoned with, as she disappeared around the corner with her sleeping bundle.

At least the identity of the mystery caller was solved.

"Alan used words like that about me all the time." She blew a stray strand of hair out of her eyes with a little bit more force than she needed. "He said I was too much, always charging ahead with things, taking over, doing things my way. I guess that's what he meant. Maybe he thought I wouldn't be a proper, obedient wife."

"I can't imagine that." He set the groceries on the counter. He couldn't say he thought much of this Alan fellow. "You are a force to be reckoned with."

"I can only be true to who I am." Her face fell, breaking him to the core.

"I meant it as a compliment, Karenna. I can't thank you enough for being you and for what you've done for us." *For me...* He kept that part to himself.

"That means a lot, Gage. You have done a lot for me, too."

"That doesn't seem likely."

"Trust me." She spun away, mindful of the sleeping child in her arms, and said no more as she disappeared from his sight.

He listened as a few of the stairs creaked beneath Karenna's sneakers. The baby apparently didn't wake, because Gage didn't hear a single gurgle as he began unloading the cold items into the fridge.

Strange how he could sense her movements upstairs. Maybe it was the faintest sound drifting down from the second story—the squeak of a door, the rasp of a catch, the whisper of her footfalls on the carpet—but somehow he felt her approach. He turned toward her before she rounded the corner and blew into sight.

Yes, he had definitely let her way past his comfort zone.

"He's down for the count," she said of Matthew.

"I want to talk about Alan." He wanted to know what was said. He folded an emptied grocery sack and slid it into the recycling bin. "Let me guess. He wanted you back."

"How did you know?"

Because I would, if I were him. He had to bite his bottom lip to keep from saying it. Would she go back? He couldn't tell by watching her. She perched at the counter on tiptoe, head bent to her task of emptying one of the sacks. He sidled closer to her to take a package of pasta to the pantry, and jealousy hit him so hard, he nearly lost his balance.

First Bucky, now the ex-fiancé. Gage shook his head, yanked open the pantry door and blindly shoved the package onto one of the shelves. He was shaking, sweating—and his stomach had coiled into one big knot. A strange urge was overtaking him, one to forbid Karenna to have anything to do with the man. He hated the thought of her marrying someone who didn't appreciate her, who had the audacity to think she wasn't great just the way she was. His ears were ringing, so it took him a second to realize she was saying something.

"I can't do it. I can't go back to him." A tomato nearly rolled out of her hands. She caught it in time and set it with several others on the counter. "I used to think I knew what I wanted in a husband. I had the picture in my head of how perfect he should be."

"And how your life was supposed to go once you found him?"

"Yes." She pulled out several small bags of fresh herbs. "You were the same way when you met your wife?"

"I would be lying if I didn't say yes, although I don't

want to admit it. I was looking for an ideal, too. Trouble was, life isn't ideal and people aren't perfect. Not even close." He took the empty bag and folded it. "What? Why are you looking at me that way, as if I'm not even close to perfect. Believe me, I already know it."

"That's not why I was smiling."

"Then why?" He leaned against the counter, towering over her like everything good and right in the world, everything a fine man ought to be.

And he was. Her mind scrambled, simply from being so near to him. She could barely think. She'd entered the mesmerizing zone that surrounded him and she'd been sucked in by the gravitational field. He had dangerous eyes, soulful and caring. What woman could resist that? Any woman would be awestruck by him.

No wonder she was in love with him.

"I was thinking I'm going to have to get a new nickname for you." She turned off the faucet and began unwrapping the packet of fresh basil.

"You have a nickname for me?"

"Well, a few. Mr. Bitter. Mr. Curmudgeon. Mr. Grinch. But now I'm thinking of calling you Mr. Perfect."

"Sarcasm? I didn't know you had it in you." He laughed at that, stalking away from her, amused.

If only she had been kidding, but she wasn't. Not even close. She carefully rinsed the leaves under running water.

"I'm going to unload the Jeep and start taping up the apartment. Maybe I can get a couple rooms done before dark." He grabbed an apple from a bowl on the table. "If you move in next door, we're going to be neighbors. This is a bad idea. What was I thinking?"

"That you're going to have to put up with me more

than you already do. I've been told I'm a lot to deal with," she quipped.

"I can handle it." He winked on his way out the door. The screen whispered shut behind him, leaving her alone in the kitchen with the rising tide of her affections and a love she prayed she could keep hidden.

He was absolutely getting too attached to her. It was all Gage could think about as he tore strip after strip of tape and lined windows and woodwork, dug out his tools to uncap light switches and take down light fixtures, and shook out the tarps he'd bought to protect Gran's furniture. All afternoon while he worked, the image taunted him of Karenna in the kitchen laughing over his nicknames. Mr. Perfect. *Really!* He chuckled in memory as he pried open a paint can lid. He was as far from perfect as any man could get.

But Karenna—she was perfection. As he filled the tray with paint, he caught a glimpse of her through the window. With Matthew on her hip, her hair tied back in a ponytail, she looked as refreshing as a summer's morning. She carried a glass of iced tea across the shaded deck and placed it on the patio table, talking all the while over her shoulder.

Her splash of liquid gold hair, her turquoise shirt and matching capris, the glint of her wristwatch, brightened in tone, until she stood out like a single spot of color in a black-and-white photograph. The blooming flowers, the forest and mountains in the background, took second fiddle to her beauty, fading away until she was all he saw. His heartbeat knocked against his ribs, his knees went shaky, and still, all he could see was her.

A trickle of fear shivered through him. These were

not friendly feelings, but something more hazardous. What had he been thinking, letting her close?

Gran caught his attention, lean and frail, waving her hand as if to brush away Karenna's concern. Gran looked pale; he could see it from a distance. She'd worked too hard today. Karenna tugged out a cushioned chair and patted it, her chin up, her stance resolute. Gran gave in with a shrug of her shoulders, crossed to the table and settled into the chair.

Good for Karenna. He backed away, drowning in gratitude, and filled the roller tray. The sharp smell of paint permeated the hot, humid air as he began to work. With each swipe, the coil in his midsection tightened.

He couldn't be falling in love with her, could he?

No. Denial kicked like an irritated donkey. He didn't do love. He refused to ever be in love. In truth, he didn't think he could ever feel that much again. At least, not with the broken pieces leftover inside him. He was no longer whole.

He knew the moment she stepped into the apartment. The rush and spatter of the paint against the wallboard had covered the pad of her gait, so it wasn't her footstep that alerted him but something else. It was like a touch of healing in his soul.

"I can't believe you've done all of this already." She sounded a little bit dazed as she stopped in the doorway. Her china-blue eyes were wide, her peaches-and-cream complexion blushed delicately with delight. She was like life itself, joyful and irresistible. "You're spoiling everything."

"I am? How?" He swiped the roller one more time across the wall, covering the last corner of the kitchen wall.

"I planned to come out tomorrow morning and help

you, but you're going to have the entire apartment done by nightfall."

"No, just the kitchen and eating area." He couldn't help envying the man who did win her heart. What a good feeling it would be to earn the reward of her smile and her easy cheer at the end of a day. He dragged the roller over a splotch of still-wet paint to even it out.

"I have dinner almost ready. Your grandmother volunteered to come tell you, but I wanted to do the honors. Mostly because I made her lie down for a quick nap for a few minutes, and wanted her to stay there. Can you believe she weeded all the flowerbeds in the entire front yard while we were in town?"

"Thanks for taking care of her." He lost his grip on the handle and the roller splashed back into the paint pan. It was easier to study the light-yellow paint than her. He didn't know what he felt, but he couldn't seem to stop it. Maybe it was the culmination of years loneliness and of not letting anyone, even Gran, get close. That *could* be the reason he was overwhelmed by a show of friendship and kindness. Then again, maybe not—and that idea unsettled him.

"Leave a plate in the oven for me," he ground out, more gruff than he meant to. "I want to finish this room before I stop to eat."

"I'll put a salad in the fridge for you, too." She didn't seem to notice he'd practically barked at her. "Are you thirsty? I can get you some lemonade before I go."

"You're leaving?"

"It's six o'clock. Time to go home. I've cleaned up the kitchen, so there's only a few plates for her to put in the dishwasher. Matthew's bathed and changed for bed." She leaned against the doorjamb. "I promised the reverend's wife that I would help her tonight."

"Are there big goings-on at the church?"

"No, but we're baking pies for a singles event tomorrow night."

"Hoping to find the real Mr. Perfect?"

"No, but I want to help the Michaelses." Once, she would have jumped for the chance to be introduced to so many of Treasure Creek's most eligible bachelors. But now? Not so much. She didn't have to meet the men to know they couldn't possibly compare to Gage. "The Michaelses are being so kind about letting me stay with them. They've refused rent of any kind."

"I'm not surprised. Edward and Jenny are good people." He filled the roller in the tray, head bent to his task, impossible to read. "Feels like a thunderstorm's brewing. You want to get home before it hits."

"Then good night, Gage. I'll see you in the morning."

"No you won't. Tomorrow is your day off."

"I know." She felt hollow as she broke away.

I wish I didn't love him, she thought later, after she'd hugged Jean goodbye and was navigating her car down the driveway. It would be easier if they were friends. Because then, every time he was friendly to her instead of loving, it wouldn't be a disappointment.

Maybe this was a rebound thing. At least she could hope so, because that would mean what she felt for Gage would be a passing thing. A sign that she was moving on and healing from her wedding fiasco.

Yes, maybe that's exactly what this was, she decided, as clouds crowded out the glare of the sun. A rebound. With every passing mile, the more certain she was of it. This was a harmless crush, nothing more.

A mile outside of town, her phone rang. "Hello?"

A garbled string of static answered. She glanced at the call screen. No name or number appeared. *Please, don't let this be Alan,* she thought, and dropped her phone back into her purse. It didn't ring again until she pulled into the Michaelses' driveway and parked behind the reverend's car.

"Hello?"

Only static again. No number. Maybe it was Maryann, calling to talk her into coming back home, or one of her sisters, to talk her into reconsidering Alan's plea.

Raindrops fell like pellets the moment she stepped out of her car.

"Can you believe this storm?" Edward Michaels hiked into sight with the day's mail under his arm. "I heard thunder a second ago. Look, there's another lightning bolt. Closer this time."

Thunder cannoned overhead and echoed across the underbelly of the black, ominous clouds.

"We'd best get inside." The reverend waited for her to go up the steps first, and onto the porch. By the time she pulled open the door, rain cascaded off the porch roof like a flooding river.

"I hope everyone we know is indoors safe and sound." Edward closed the door, cutting off the chill of the harsh wind.

"Me, too." Karenna thought of Gage in the little apartment over his garage. She knew he was still painting, probably things like a severe storm didn't bother him. What would it be like to be iron tough and nothing could touch you?

She wished she knew how to be like that; that way she would be in control of the love she felt for him. That way she could make it fade away all the faster.

"Good, there you two are." Jenny popped around the

corner, wearing an apron over her pantsuit and sporting a mixing bowl in the crook of one arm. "Karenna, did you have a good day? Come tell me all about it while we bake."

Chapter Eleven

Saturday morning dawned pristine and peaceful, the air clean from the rain, all traces of storm gone from the sky. Gage took a sip of coffee, propped his ankles on the deck rail and watched the golden light filter through the tree tops, christening everything. This is what he needed—a moment's peace to mull over what was troubling him.

Denial wasn't doing the job for him—he'd gone to sleep with her on his mind and he woke the same way. Going over and over the images of her from the previous day—blessed by the morning light as she tumbled out of her car, intently mopping the apartment floor while she hummed, seated on the bench in town, her head bent as if in sadness. He lingered over every detail and every nuance, trying to stem emotions too dangerous to feel. He couldn't go there, he couldn't allow it. He put the brakes on his sentiments and tried to purge those dear images of her from his mind.

No good.

The emotion—okay, it *was* affection—remained, stubbornly lodged deep in his chest. He didn't want to examine it. If he ignored it, maybe it would go away and he would never have to let the affection he felt for Karenna have power over him.

A final image flashed into his thoughts. Karenna standing in the yard with the baby in one arm, radiating happiness. An unbidden, impossible wish took root in his soul.

No! He ordered it out, squeezed his eyes shut and forced his mind to clear. No way could he start picturing a future between him and Karenna that could not exist. Even the thought tore at him. He could not face the agony of trusting another woman like that again.

I can't see that happening, he reached out in prayer. Was God listening to him these days? He didn't know, but he didn't know where else to turn. *Can You see it, Father?*

He didn't expect an answer. Birdsong peppered the morning's stillness, and Gage considered heading back for a second cup of coffee before getting off his duff. The apartment wasn't going to paint itself.

Something broke the peace. A bluejay squawked and took flight, cutting low across the back lawn and the poled green beans spiking up behind the garden gate. Tires crunched on the gravel driveway and the rumble of a badly timed engine chugged closer. He didn't have to get out of his chair to know there would be a faded purple Fiat rolling into view. He knew it was Karenna by the panic bursting to life inside him.

Being around her was like climbing a cliff without tie lines. All he could do was pray he didn't fall.

She climbed out of her car. Wearing pink today. A backpack was slung over her shoulder, and the teabag label dangling from the travel coffee mug she carried swung in rhythm with her snappy gait.

"You look comfy," she commented.

"Just enjoying the morning."

"I never thought I would see Gage Parker loafing around." She hopped onto the deck. "It's seven o'clock and you're not out and about yet."

"I am now." He launched out of the deck chair like a rocket. Good thing the mug was empty or he would have spilled it. "I thought we agreed you had the day off. You don't work weekends."

"*I* didn't remember agreeing, and it doesn't matter, since I'm here as a friend." She kept coming, advancing without fear or invitation. "You know what friends are, right? A buddy. A pal."

"I don't remember agreeing to that. You're the one who is all buddy-buddy." He definitely couldn't categorize his feelings as friendly. Not now, and he suspected, not ever again. He yanked open the screen door, needing to put some distance between them. "You aren't going to help with the painting."

"You say that as if you are judge and jury."

"I am. It *is* my apartment."

"Yes, but you're going to let me live there."

"A bad decision at the time. See how important it is to consider the consequences before you make up your mind about something?"

"Your grandmother was right. You *do* have a sense of humor."

Did she have to be so pleased about it? Did she have to be so breathtaking? If she was underfoot all day long, cooped up in that small apartment alone with him, how could he keep his feelings for her under control? Every time he was near her, it was like a swift-moving current pulling him down the river.

Just think of Gran and Matthew, he told himself. That's why he had invited her to stay in the first place.

"I'm not joking about this," he insisted. "I can handle the painting."

"But I'm already here."

"You drove all this way, you can drive back."

"But I want to help."

"I don't want you to."

"Has anyone ever told you that you are a very stubborn man?"

"Dozens of people. Maybe hundreds." The corners of his mouth struggled to stay downturned, the only hint of his true opinion on the matter.

"Unfortunately for you, I am not like those other people." She breezed into the kitchen and dropped her keys and backpack by the back door. "I don't frustrate easily."

"I don't believe you." He poured another cup of coffee. "I'm calling your bluff."

"What bluff?"

"I seem to remember a young woman in a wedding dress kicking her car tire." Amusement transformed him, and it was simple to see the man who'd once been described as always laughing. "You looked incredibly frustrated then."

"An entirely rare occurrence." She rolled her eyes. He *would* have to mention it. "I was under extreme duress. Why do you keep bringing that up?"

"So I don't like you too much."

"I know the feeling, Mr. Stubborn."

"Not Mr. Perfect?" He leaned against the counter, watching her over his cup.

"That's entirely up to you, and judging by your mood this morning, no." She had to tease him, right? Because there was no way she could admit that, at this exact moment, he was beyond perfect. He was a wish she hadn't dreamed until this moment. "I can be just as stubborn. I *am* helping you, right after I get breakfast ready for Jean and maybe you, if you're nice."

"So, what's for breakfast?"

"Egg-white omelets, fresh fruit, bran-banana muffins and turkey bacon."

"I suppose I can survive all this healthy eating. As long as you don't try and take my coffee away from me."

"Even I am not that brave," she quipped. She adored the way his eyes warmed to a blueberry color when his guard went down. "Now, out of my kitchen. I have work to do."

He took his steaming coffee cup, saluted her with it and escaped outside, but the bubble of happiness in her chest remained unbreakable.

"You missed a spot." Karenna set down her roller, placed her hands on her hips and swiveled, hoping to stretch the kink out of her back. They'd been painting for most of the day, and the dingy living space had transformed into a cheerful, pleasant dwelling. Add a little lace and ruffled curtains and it would be a perfect hideaway.

"Where?" Gage ran his roller through the paint in the pan and squinted at the sunny wall.

"Halfway up, about six inches from the corner. The sun is shining on it. You probably can't see it from your angle."

He probably had no idea how appealing he was, with tiny paint splatters polka-dotting his gray T-shirt. A streak of pale yellow smeared his cheek. She couldn't remember any man she'd seen in her entire life who was so *it*—so manly, vital and awesome. Gage Parker didn't look the part—he was the genuine article. Be still, her heart.

"Right here?" He held the roller up to the wall, not touching it, glancing over his wide shoulder for confirmation.

"An inch my way."

"That would be seven inches." The crook of his grin ought to be studied as a work of art.

"Fine. Seven inches. Like I have a ruler. As if."

That made him laugh, a deep, rumbling chuckle that made the day brighten.

This is just a rebound thing, she told herself. Maybe if she said it enough, she could make it into the truth. She pried the tape off the door frame and pulled, and the length came free. In all, it had been a fun day spent with Gage, even if it was a lot of hard work.

"What do you think?" He stood back, roller in hand.

"I think it's safe to say we are officially finished."

"Good. I think this looks all right. I hardly recognize the place."

"You did a great job painting. You work fast." She wadded the tape into a ball and gave it a toss. It stuck to her fingers, so she had to walk it to the trash bag.

"The two of us made quick work of it." He laid down his roller in the empty paint tray. "You are a mess."

"I know." She managed to get the tape into the bag, but her fingers were sticky with tacky paint. That wasn't the worst of it, not by far. The old T-shirt she'd worn sported tiny spatters of paint. Pink and yellow speckled the gray background like Easter gone wild. "Trouble finds me."

"More like you find trouble." Gage ripped a paper towel off the roll and wet it, shaking his head. "Have you always been like this?"

"Yes, I keep trying to change my ways, but it doesn't seem to work." Now she was babbling to cover up her nerves. He was stalking toward her like a cougar stalked a rabbit and she stayed the urge to run.

"Guess you'll be going to the church thing tonight?" He came around the edge of the counter.

"Church thing?" Her brain didn't click into gear. His nearness muddled her thinking. "Oh, you mean the singles Meet and Greet?"

"I reckon the reverend and his wife figured on doing their part to unite the bachelors of Treasure Creek with some of the new ladies in town?" So close now, she could see the texture of his five-o'clock shadow on his jaw.

"I suppose so." Her throat had gone dry. "You must know the Michaelses pretty well."

"I've been a member of Treasure Creek Christian Church for as long as I can remember." Honesty crinkled handsomely in the corners of his eyes as he cradled her chin in his wide palm. "Not that I've been attending much lately."

"Lately?" Overwhelmed, she couldn't focus. He towered over her, filling her field of vision, his touch holding her captive by its gentleness.

"I feel like a hypocrite when I sit on a pew, so I stopped going."

"How long ago was this?"

"A while." He did his best to keep his hurt from showing, but she recognized it.

"Since you came back to Treasure Creek."

His silence answered for him. Nothing about Gage

Parker appeared tender as he towered over her, blocking the fall of light. But as he swiped at her cheek with a damp paper towel, he could be described as nothing but.

With his feet planted and braced apart, he could have been a lumberjack or a fully clothed, paint-spattered wrestler about to take the mat, except for a corresponding kindness on his face. No scowl, no frown, no harsh look. His forehead furrowed as he worked swabbing paint from her cheek. With his guard down, this was the true Gage Parker.

Irresistible.

"Done." He studied her a moment longer, his gaze tracking across the bridge of her nose.

He was probably noticing her freckles. Her stomach went quivery as his gaze stroked her cheeks like a touch, along the tip of her nose and the length of her mouth. He paused for a nanosecond. Her pulse skipped with a dash of shock. Was he going to kiss her?

"Looks like there's one more spot." The paper towel rasped against her skin. "And another."

"I can get it," she said, breathlessly.

"No need." He dabbed at her chin, the edge of the towel brushing the outline of her mouth. "Just one more."

"Painting is messy business."

"Yes it is." He tackled the last spec of paint on her chin, fighting with himself. He wanted to kiss her. He wanted to draw her to his chest. He needed to know what it would be like to cradle her tenderly in his arms.

Not going to happen. He backed away, casually putting distance between them, hoping he didn't look like a man besotted. He hoped his battle for willpower didn't show as he tossed the balled-up paper towel into the garbage sack.

"There. Now you're presentable." His voice became thick, not sounding at all like his own. Would she notice?

Hard to say if she did. He should have pulled back, kept his guard up and distance between them. Too late now.

"Come with me tonight." Hope animated her.

As if she wasn't cute enough. "I don't know, Karenna."

"C'mon. It will be a lot of fun."

"I don't like to have fun."

"You aren't fooling me one bit." She tilted her head, her ponytail tumbling over her shoulder, her soft bangs brushing the face that had become most precious to him. "You are scared by the fact it's a singles event."

"That's not my thing." Never had he had such a hard time standing his ground. He loved Edward and his wife. They were great people. He'd been to many singles events at the church before he'd left for college and a different life. He'd had optimism then—and faith. No optimism remained.

"Please. Everyone is going to be there. Think of all the friends you could catch up with."

Why her? No other woman had ever affected him like this, and he didn't like it. Worse, he didn't know how to stop it. He feared there was no way to keep his affections for her from taking flight.

"I'm sure you know plenty of the townspeople who will be there," she went on, unaware of his struggle. She grabbed the paint pan and roller she'd been using, and carried it to the door. "If you come tonight, you can meet all the women who haven't taken a tour with you yet."

"Now you're trying to marry me off?" Anger tore through him as he grabbed his paint tray and followed her into the warm kiss of the wind.

"Well, I hadn't thought of that. Do you think there's a chance someone might take a fancy to you?"

"I hope not." He stumbled down the steps after her, drawn by her in a way he could not explain. He didn't care about other women. What he cared about was her.

"You just never know when love will hook you." Karenna seemed to be taking great delight in ribbing him. "You don't know what God has in store for you."

"I had a pretty good idea when I signed my divorce papers. Some men aren't made for marriage."

"You don't believe that, do you?" Her hand curled around his, so small and soft, and something hitched in his chest—a great swell of affection he could not stop.

"God may not be done with you yet." She continued on. "There may be great good meant to come into your life."

I wish it could be you. The thought ravaged him. Karenna had changed him. He liked to think he was a man who wasn't hopeless. That he still had some good left inside him.

"Since when is marriage a great good?" He jested to keep things light.

"Not funny." She disappeared into the shadows of the garage. "I can't blame you, after what happened."

"Do you mean my marriage? I never told you about Margaret." He dropped his tray and roller in the industrial sink. "Gran talked, didn't she?"

"She may have mentioned a few things about your divorce."

"What things?" He hit the faucet and ran the roller through the stream.

"You came back to Alaska devastated." Understanding made her voice rich, interwoven with layers of sympathy and concern.

"She told you I was devastated?" he ground out. "I was *not* devastated. I was annoyed. Inconvenienced."

"Sure. I understand."

"Margaret didn't matter that much to me, not in the end." *She would never understand,* he thought, *because it hadn't happened to her.* Maybe women didn't love the way men did. They were too busy seeing a paycheck and figuring out a way to get the house they wanted and couldn't afford. In Margaret's eyes, he had largely been like a department store Santa Claus with a magic, no-limit credit card.

Maybe Karenna was different—he had learned that much about her. But she wasn't exactly coming at marriage realistically. She wanted the dream—happy marriage, loving family, security and comfort. Who didn't?

But it was a myth, a fairy tale, fiction that had no place in the real world.

"Tell me what happened." She set her pan next to his in the sink, her hand landing on his shoulder in sympathy. "I won't say a single word. I'll just listen."

"I never talk about it." He grabbed her roller and rinsed it under the faucet, watching watery paint stream out. He was careful not to look up, not to see her, not to see anything.

"Never?" she asked.

How could a single voice impart so much caring? He

squeezed his eyes shut momentarily, fighting a losing battle—one that never could be won.

The truth spilled out. "She said I was distant. I never saw how. I was always there for her. I was *there*. In the same room. In the same house. Sharing a life."

True to her word, Karenna remained silent. He felt as if all of her listened as he set the pans to soak. Her hand remained on his shoulder, a blaze of comfort. Fine, so he was grateful for it. He'd kept everything bottled up for too long, and he trusted Karenna with the truth.

"I gave her everything I had. Everything I was capable of. And it wasn't enough." He pumped liquid soap into his hands and scrubbed at the paint dried to his skin. Blotches of color came off. If only he could transform his life as easily, to wash away the real Gage Parker and find a newer and better one beneath.

"I did everything I knew how to do," he confessed, "but she left me for another man."

She didn't answer. Her silence was response enough. He could feel her compassion in the stillness between them. A connection melded them, and he could feel her spirit leaning to his. He no longer felt alone. The old wounds no longer felt raw and impossible to heal.

"Come with me tonight, Gage. I could use a friend."

He grabbed a towel and rubbed at the wetness on his hands and arms. Oh, the woman had changed him. He did not want to say no to her. "It doesn't feel right to leave Gran with Matthew while I go off and play."

"That's easy. We'll take him with us."

"To a single's shindig?"

"Why not? He's single, too." She laughed, a sound radiating life, joy and everything good in the world.

Everything he had ever wanted.

He put the towel back on the bar. "I'm going to regret this."

"Oh, you are *so* not!" She clapped. "You are going to have the best time ever."

He rolled his eyes, wishing he could summon up a fierce scowl or a formidable glower. But could he?

Nope. Not so much as a frown. And it was all Karenna's fault.

"I've got to get showered and changed. Look at me. I'm covered with paint." She danced away from him, but the distance did not feel as if it separated them. It felt as if nothing could.

"I'll meet you and Matthew at the church in an hour." She stopped at the door, posing in the sunlight. "Don't be late."

"I won't," he promised, losing a piece of himself when she dashed out of his sight.

Chapter Twelve

An hour later, Karenna was freshly showered, with every speckle of paint scrubbed off, wearing a pretty, summery dress she'd picked up at the General Store, and was attempting to navigate from the Michaelses' home through the busy streets. A three-ring circus set up in the middle of town wouldn't be as interesting as Treasure Creek Lane.

The main street was crammed with tourists, and the festive cheer in the air was contagious, as she waited in a long, unmoving line of cars. She twisted in her seat to see what the problem was. It looked like up ahead a rental car was squeezing out of what had to be the only available parking spot curbside anywhere. People crossed the street and ambled down sidewalks, many of them women appearing to head down the street toward the church.

As interesting as it all was, nothing had been able to tempt her away from remembering her afternoon with Gage. *I gave her everything I had. Everything I was capable of. And it wasn't enough.* His confession stayed with her, the heartbreak in his words compelling and real. It blew her away that he'd trusted her enough to open up and share what had to be one of the most painful experiences of his life. She knew how vulnerable love could make a person, because that's where she was right now.

Vulnerable. She hit her blinker, waiting patiently in line behind a long queue of cars. It looked as if they were all waiting to get into the church lot. She frowned at both the wait and the undeniable fact that what she felt for Gage wasn't rebound love.

No, this was something much more than she had ever known before. She felt a little panicky because she would be seeing him in a few minutes. It felt almost like a date, the start of something new and great.

But what if she was getting ahead of herself? She had a tendency to look before she leaped. What if Gage wasn't ready? After his confession, was he regretting opening up to her? Had he realized he would never be ready to risk everything in another relationship?

Her cell phone came to life with a startling ring, just as she slipped into one of the last free spots in the Treasure Creek Christian Church parking lot.

Please, don't let that be Gage cancelling on me. Her stomach squeezed as she fished the phone out of her purse. She checked the readout, expecting the worst, but it wasn't Gage's number. It was one she recognized, however. How interesting. "Hi, Maryann. I'm surprised it took you this long to get back to me."

"I've been trying to call you for days, but the reception in Alaska can be patchy."

"Tell me about it." She loved her cousin, but she wasn't exactly in the mood to receive a single-is-good pep talk. "It has been useful in avoiding your calls."

"I knew it." Maryann didn't seem upset about it. "I need to talk with you, Karenna."

"Don't even bother trying to talk me into going back to Seattle. If that's why you've called, then you are wasting your time." Honestly, she adored her cousin, but she didn't need saving.

"If you would listen, then I could tell you I'm not calling from California." She paused, her voice quivering with purpose. "I'm here."

"What? Where?" Karenna pulled the key from the ignition.

"I'm in Treasure Creek."

"Alaska?" No way. "You have a dry sense of humor, cousin."

"No, really. Since you wouldn't listen to reason, I decided to bring reason to you."

There wasn't an ounce of humor in Maryann's voice. Not a hint of teasing. Surely, her sensible and antimarriage cousin wasn't serious? She hauled her purse off the passenger seat, hooked the strap over her shoulder and gave the rusty door a good slam. "So let me get this straight. You're coming to Treasure Creek? Don't tell me you've come to check out the handsome bachelors, too?"

"Don't be silly. Of course not. This is about you." Maryann sounded dead serious. "I'm driving through the center of town right now."

"Through *this* town?" That was impossible.

"Yes. You didn't answer my question. Where are you?"

Wow, maybe she really was here. A black SUV turned into the lot. Gage. She brightened inside, glad he'd come for her. "Look up. Do you see a church steeple anywhere?"

"Right in the center of town."

"I'm in the parking lot." She returned Gage's wave when his black SUV eased into the parking space next to her. She wanted to wait for him, but she was already running, sneakers squeaking against the pavement and holding tightly to her phone. "What are you driving?"

"A blue rental car. I can't believe this place. It's like something out of a movie."

"Don't you love it?" She was excited now, bounding around people and springing out onto the sidewalk. She felt Gage's gaze like a brand on her back. She spun around to catch sight of him, hungry for a glimpse of him, but a blue sedan sitting in line to turn into the lot caught her attention.

It really was Maryann!

"Go around and park on the street!" Karenna spoke into her phone and pointed beyond the line of cars to an empty space half a block ahead. She glanced over her shoulder, but couldn't see Gage. He may be out of her sight, but she could feel him as if by heart.

You are going to have to face the truth, she told herself. *You are seriously, no-holds-barred in love with him.* But what she could do about it remained a mystery.

"I hope you aren't at the church for a wedding," Maryann commented, the phone crackling. "As in *your* wedding."

"No, don't be silly. My wedding is tomorrow," she quipped.

"What? Karenna, is that a joke?" Maryann didn't sound as if she approved of that sort of humor. "It's not a very good one. And if it's not, then I've arrived just in time."

Oh, she had missed her cousin more than she realized. Laughing, she jogged along the sidewalk, waiting impatiently while Maryann parked in a narrow spot. The moment the door opened, she gave a shout of glee and wrapped her cousin into a welcoming, joyful hug.

Karenna's shout of joy sailed across the street and the parking lot, somehow floating above the other noises as car doors slammed, conversations rose and fell, folks called out in greeting. Gage flung open the passenger-side door, where Matthew began squealing, arms stretched out, excited to be picked up.

He ignored the boy for a moment. His every sense was tuned to Karenna. She'd bounded away from him pretty fast, without so much as giving him a wave. And now the sound of her shout was the one he could pick out in the noisy parking lot. That went to show how tuned-in he was to her. He didn't have to search across the crowded lot. His gaze automatically found her.

Where was she going? And—worse—what was she up to?

He reached in to unbuckle Matthew. His gaze remained fixed on her. Golden hair flying, jumping with joy, she flung her arms out and raced around the back of a parked car, excited to see someone.

What if that was her fiancé? Fear jackhammered through him. A pickup blocked his view. He couldn't see who it was she'd wrapped into a hug. He squeezed his eyes shut, unwilling to witness the moment when the truck moved and he saw her in the arms of another man. Proof that she wasn't his. She never had been. Would never be.

"Ahhh!" Matthew commented cheerfully.

"I'll get you out, buddy." He got to work unbuckling the boy, keeping his gaze on Matthew and only on Matthew.

"Let's say her fiancé does want her back. You know she's going to marry him, or someone else," he told the boy. "I don't know why I'm tangled up about this."

"Eeee!"

"You're right. I never had a chance with her. Time to be realistic." If only he could will his chest to stop hurting so much. It was ridiculous.

He wasn't hurting over some woman. Maybe it was from inhaling too many paint fumes. That must be it. All those chemicals in the paint. He hadn't acted himself. He'd wanted to kiss her. Worse, he'd opened up to her. Regret filled him. Not that he was sorry, but he'd been too vulnerable. He wasn't the sort of man who went around letting just anyone close.

The reason had to be those paint chemicals. They effected his brain. It wasn't his iron defenses weakening around her. It wasn't because he cared too much for her.

"Oh!" Matthew clapped his hands to get attention, the cute little guy. Gage fought feeling warmth for the boy because he knew Ryan. His brother would be back eventually, and leave taking Matthew, so it made no sense getting attached.

Face it, life was easier if you didn't make emotional ties. No ties, then no devastation when those ties unraveled.

"You ready to meet Karenna's ex?" He tucked the baby's weight in one arm and shut the door. Matthew leaned into him, cuddling close, and shouted out a few words of gleeful babble.

"I'll take that as a yes." He wished he could say the

same. He turned his shoulder, to keep the rest of the parking lot out of his field of vision in case Karenna and her Alan were embracing. The idea sent shards of agony into his chest.

Boy, those paint fumes really must have got to him. Good thing he was tough and unfeeling, or he would be in a whole lot of hurt right now. He kept his head down and his gaze planted on the walkway ahead of him.

"Gage!" Karenna called out, the melody of her voice making him turn toward her against his will.

Brace yourself. This is going to hurt, but you can handle it. He set his jaw and steeled his spine.

"Come meet my cousin." She bounded onto the walkway in front of him, joyful and full of life. She dazzled.

Every troubled place within him stilled.

"Cousin?" Not the fiancé? He blinked at the pretty woman with pale brown eyes standing beside Karenna. She had a dark bob and fringy bangs.

He couldn't believe it. He'd gotten all worked up for nothing. Had he been brave enough to have waited a few seconds and taken a good look, he would have noticed right off that Karenna was greeting a woman, not his imagined nemesis.

"Hello, handsome." Karenna's gaze dropped to his chest, where the baby was jabbering at her. "Will you be my date to the singles party?"

"Eeee!"

The women laughed, enchanted by the baby. But he was in a free fall. There was no way to explain the pounding in his head, the mixed-up emotions that knotted him up or the deep longing for what he could never have again.

He handed over the infant, feeling the brush of Karenna's hand against his own and doing his best to ignore that, too.

"Maryann won't admit it, but she came to check out all the handsome bachelors in this town." Karenna sparkled with mischief, riveting him.

How she could sneak past his defenses and hold him captive remained a mystery. When he knew he ought to step away, he couldn't.

"I certainly did not," her cousin protested, causing Karenna to laugh.

All he could see was her. Her dazzle, her spirit, her goodness shining like the most precious of jewels.

"Maryann says she came to save me from myself, and that would be just like her. She's a nurse. She saves people all the time." Karenna twirled with a flare of her skirt and sauntered up to the walkway to the church.

"I did come here to save you from yourself." Maryann seemed like a sensible woman. She saw a banner and stopped to read it. "What is going on here? This is a singles event. You tricked me, Karenna."

"I didn't trick you. When I invited you to come with me, I simply didn't mention the place would be full of single men."

"I see more single women than I do men."

"This is Alaska." She held out her hand. "C'mon, Gage. I want to meet your high-school friends so I can hear old stories about you that you don't want me to know."

Danger, his instincts warned. Red alert. Nothing could be more hazardous than Karenna. He didn't want to admit it, but he could no longer hide from the truth. When he'd thought she was greeting Alan and he was about to lose her, it felt as if his world could have ended. That his already broken heart would take another fatal blow.

Could he afford to risk another?

His feet felt heavy, as if to drag him backward instead of along the walkway that led behind the church. A step ahead of him, Karenna walked side-by-side with her cousin, chatting merrily, and beyond them was a crowd on the cool lawn, the din of conversation buzzing in his head like a swarm of flies.

He wanted her. He couldn't have her. He didn't believe in love that much.

"Gage!"

He turned at the familiar voice, relieved to have a reason not to head into the crowd. He needed time away from Karenna. He needed to clear his head and to think. Jake Rodgers broke out of the crowd with a sense of urgency.

Gage fell back, figuring Karenna was busy with her cousin. Sure enough, the minister's wife approached them, took Matthew into her arms and warmly greeted Maryann. Sensing girl talk, he spun on his heel, wondering what was up with his friend.

"Your grandmother said I could find you here." Troubled, Jake didn't bother with small talk. He got right to the point. "I just got off the phone with Reed and spotted your rig in the lot, so I came over. Figure your phone will be ringing—"

As if on cue, the cell in his pocket chimed. That could only mean one thing. Someone was lost and he was being called out. He flipped open the phone. "Gage here."

"It's Reed. Gear up. What's your ETA?"

"I'm in town, and my gear's in the back of my Jeep." Judging by the worry in the chief's tone and the concern furrowed on Jake's face, this was serious, and, he knew in his gut, personal. Someone they all knew and cared about was missing.

"Then head on over. I've got the county's chopper arriving in ten."

"A chopper?" For a local search-and-rescue? That could mean someone got into trouble in the mountains or—

"We've got reports that Tucker's plane didn't arrive. He fell out of the sky and we're going to find him."

"Roger that." Gage pocketed his phone. A bad feeling dug into his gut. He saw the knowledge on Jake's face, the fear neither of them wanted to say out loud. Small-plane crashes did not turn out well, more often than not. He'd been on several recovery missions—all fatalities. His throat closed up. He couldn't stand to think of their good friend Tucker meeting that kind of end.

"We've got to think positively." Jake set his jaw, as if determined to will a better outcome.

"Right." Gage clapped his old friend on the back, in silent understanding. They'd watched out for one another, the three of them. That's what friends did. Not every bond was something that weakened over time. Friendship was something a man could count on. "I'll meet you at the station?"

"Roger that." Jake strode away, focused on the upcoming mission. A rescue—God willing—and not a recovery.

Look out for Tucker, Lord. Gage put all his might in the prayer. *Please let him be all right.*

He hoped heaven could hear him. He needed heaven to hear him. He'd been groping along in his life, without faith, without a scrap of anything he felt he could believe in. He felt like a drowning man going down for the final time.

He opened his eyes and the noise of the crowd echoed crazily in his ears. All the faces were blurs. Hard to focus on anything when his entire being felt ready to crack apart. He spotted Karenna up ahead in the crowd, Matthew back in her arms as she introduced her cousin to a group of women he didn't know. Falling for her had been a precarious thing. He'd almost tumbled right into that trap. But this emergency call was heaven-sent. He had no doubt about that. The Lord was giving him a clear sign, and he was going to abide by it.

I won't love her. I can't let that happen. I have to stop it.

Maybe if he stood firm, fought with all his considerable self-control and discipline, he would be able to will the inevitable from happening. His feelings would retreat and he would be safe again.

He squeezed his eyes shut, set his jaw and turned on his heel. When he opened his eyes again, his back was to her and she was safely out of his sight, forever out of his heart.

Something tugged on his sleeve and, faintly, he heard a voice, growing louder as he focused on it.

"Is that your baby over there?" A woman had sidled up to him. "He sure is real cute. I notice you aren't wearing a wedding ring. Are you one of the bachelors the article talked about?"

"No, I am not." What had the world come to? Had everyone gone loony tunes? He understood the naive view of marriage, of having someone love you, to share your life with that person, every moment, the ups and downs, growing old together. But how desperate were these women? What kind of female left her home for parts unknown just to find a man to marry? Apparently any man would do. Apparently the high possibility of a future divorce didn't worry them any.

"Excuse me." He wrenched away from the woman, wove furiously around a hungry circle of them.

"Yoo-hoo! I'm so happy you came!" A woman bounced to a stop before him, halting his progress toward the door. "I've been dying to thank you for saving my life."

"Huh?" It took a few seconds for the fuzz his mind had become to clear enough to remember the clueless miss he'd climbed down a cliff to rescue. That had been the night Karenna had come to town.

Karenna. His gaze shot through the crowd, searching for her. Finding her again was like an undercurrent pulling him down. He couldn't breathe. He was helpless to stop the rush of devotion he did not want to feel.

"So, thank you. Now you're my very own hero." A voice came as if from far away. The woman flashed him a smile. "Would you like to grab a cup of punch? There's homemade desserts, too, and I hear the apple pie is to die for."

"Not in the mood." His head pounded.

"I saw your son. What a little darling. He's so cute." She tossed a lock of hair behind her shoulder. "My name is Ashley and—"

"Hope you have a good evening." He feigned left, managed to get around her, cut through the dizzying jam of single ladies of every age trying to catch his eye.

Where was Karenna? She'd drifted off, out of his line of sight. He checked his watch. He had only a few minutes to find her before he had to head over to the station. Everything within him ached for her sweet beauty and her gentle presence.

You do not love her, he told himself, as he strode into the crowd.

Chapter Thirteen

"Matthew is a total dear." Maryann took Matthew in her arms and smiled down at him. "What a good baby he is."

"He's been a joy to care for." Was she blushing? Karenna knew she was. Even the tips of her ears felt pink. "It was a blessing to find a job right away."

"You like working for these people?" Maryann's intelligent gaze sharpened. "It's different working in a private home than in a day-care center."

"I love Gage's grandmother." There she went using the L word again. How pesky of it to keep popping into her sentences. "You will have to meet Jean. She is as sweet as Grandma Olive."

"And the father? What do you think of him?"

"Gage is Matthew's uncle. The father took off a few weeks ago without any word. No one knows when he will be back. Can you imagine?" She melted. Fine, she was falling in love with the baby, too. Her arms ached for his dear weight. "Gage is—"

"Yes?" Maryann prompted.

How did she sing the man's praises without giving

away her secret? She didn't know how to sort it out, so she took a sip of the punch Maryann had just fetched for them. Where had he gone to?

"That's what I thought." Her cousin looked pleased with herself. "Now tell me all about the buried treasure."

It took considerable effort to rip her gaze away from the big crowd congregated on the church's lawn. She'd lost sight of Gage, and she felt as if something vital was missing. As if she'd somehow lost him—which made no sense. She knew he was somewhere nearby. It was simply her earlier worries still bugging her. They'd gotten close this afternoon. Maybe that meant this evening Gage would see her home, she could invite him in for tea and they could talk, really talk, just the two of them.

Maryann was watching her expectantly and Karenna had to dig into her thoughts to remember her cousin had asked a question. She shrugged. "What buried treasure? I don't know a thing about it."

"Everyone is talking about it. It's the only topic of discussion over at the punch bowl." Maryann smiled down at the baby in her arms. "Someone was talking about how they'd bought a map from someone in town and they're heading out tonight to try to hunt it down."

"This is gold country. It is exciting to think that over a hundred years ago people were rushing here, hoping to strike it rich." It wasn't material riches she had come to find, but to each his own. "Do you think it's authentic?"

"Oh, I'm a skeptic, but it is thrilling to imagine," Maryann said, with a hint of good humor. "It's as if a piece of history could come to life. I wouldn't waste good money buying a map, though."

"Me, either." She'd already found her treasure. Love lifted through her, and she longed for the sight of Gage's handsome face and the dependable strength of his presence.

"Howdy there." A middle-aged woman with big, blond hair and a friendly smile sauntered over. "We met in the store the other day. I'm Jolene."

"Yes, of course I remember. You were so friendly to me. This is my cousin, Maryann." Since it was wonderfully good to have her beloved cousin with her, she couldn't help wrapping her arm around Maryann's shoulder. "She just arrived. She says she didn't come up here to check out all the handsome bachelors."

"That can't be right? Sugar, no one could resist some of these men. I can't remember the last time I saw so many good, decent guys in one place. Maybe never. It's sure nice to meet you, Maryann."

"Nice to meet you." Maryann smiled, obviously finding it hard not to like Jolene Jones. "I was just asking Karenna about the buried treasure rumors. Do you know anything more about it? I'm curious about the history."

"Sure, I've been talkin' up a storm with lots of folks. I've got the scoop." Jolene leaned in, ready to share. "From what I've been able to find out, no one in Amy's family has ever come close to findin' the map her great-great-grandfather supposedly left behind. Word is that Amy wasn't even sure she believed it existed. Now, mind you, maybe it is nothing more than a story, grown in proportion over the years into a legend. But rumor has it the map has been found, and someone got their hands on it and made a few copies."

"That's the part that seems iffy to me," Maryann interjected. "If I were Amy and I found a real treasure map, I wouldn't let it out of my sight. So it couldn't have been copied."

"How does anyone know there really is a treasure? Maybe it was dug up long ago." Karenna studied the mountains rising up beyond town. Once they were filled with prospectors mining for their fortunes.

"That's what I wondered, too," Jolene confessed. "So I asked around until I learned more about this Mack Tanner. He was a merchant who earned his fortune in a fair and decent way, sellin' supplies and whatnot to prospectors caught up in the Alaskan gold rush. Mack didn't give in to greed, and he never took advantage of others, like a lot of other store owners did. Keep in mind, he probably made a fortune of his own, treatin' his customers fair. He buried his gold somewhere on his property adjacent to the Chilkoot Trail. Folks say it is land Amy owns now. I can just imagine a fortune in gold just waitin' all these years to be found."

"How amazing to have such a family history," Maryann said.

Karenna couldn't focus. The back of her neck tingled. She knew it was Gage before she spotted him plowing across the lawn.

His attention fastened on her as he closed the distance between them, ignoring all the single ladies who watched him admiringly. She wanted to catch him by the arm and lay claim to him so those other women would back off.

She didn't have that right.

"I need to go," he bit out, all business and intense focus. "A friend of mine is missing, and I'm going to help with the search."

"You're leaving, of course. You *must* go." Disappointment warred with pride. She'd fallen in love with a real-life hero. "You must be afraid for your friend. Has he been missing for long?"

"Long enough for it to be a real concern." He was remote again, his emotional walls were up and it was hard to see in. "Can you take Matthew home after the barbecue?"

"You don't even have to ask."

"Thanks." No emotion crossed his face. He was granite—cold, unfeeling stone. He took a step back, and a great yawning distance stretched between them. He walked away without a goodbye.

She knew he had to be sick with worry over his missing friend, but this felt personal. It felt as if he had made the decision to pull away from her.

"Oh, honey, don't tell me you've gone and fell in love, too." Jolene's hand rested on Karenna's forearm for a brief, sympathetic squeeze. "I know how that is. It's torture when you love a man who isn't ready to love you right back."

"I'm not in love with him," she denied. "Well, not *too* much."

"Darlin', you just keep tellin' yourself that." Jolene shook her head, as if she knew full well what Karenna was trying to do. If she could convince herself she wasn't in love, then she couldn't be hurt.

"This is exactly what I have been worrying about," Maryann admitted. Matthew cooed contentedly in her arms.

"Finally! Some familiar faces." A red-haired woman in designer clothes squeezed into their small circle. "Hi, Karenna. We met the other day. Jolene, I can't believe you showed up here after all."

"We are staying at the same hotel," Jolene explained. "I was thinking I might not come, seein' as I'm already sweet on a man. Then I got to thinkin' maybe he would put in an appearance, so I had to come."

"We're glad you did," Karenna added. "Delilah, of course I remember you. Have you met anyone interesting yet?"

"Not my Prince Charming. Yet." Delilah's coils of red hair bobbed gently as she talked. She was a lovely lady, dressed up as if for a social event in Beverly Hills, overdone for the casual get-together. "Say, you girls wouldn't happen to know who the most eligible bachelor in town is?"

Karenna could only think of one.

"I'll introduce you to a few," Jolene volunteered, taking Delilah by the hand. "C'mon. We'll see you girls later!"

"Bye," Karenna called out, struggling to pull her thoughts back from Gage. Not easy. Not easy at all. He'd felt so distant. He'd looked so cold, all the closeness they'd shared seemed to vanish.

"Those poor women." Maryann watched the marriage-minded ladies disappear into the crowd. "They seem nice enough, but they really don't have any idea about what matters in life."

"They are trying to find true love. Not everyone is as down on marriage as you." Karenna couldn't resist teasing. "I still can't believe you're here in Alaska."

"I would have come sooner if I hadn't gotten lost." Maryann waited while Matthew shouted, contributing to the conversation.

"Lost? What happened?"

"I could only get a flight to Anchorage, so I had to drive the rest of the way. At first, I was really unhappy about wasting all that time in a car. But the scenery is spectacular. It was all I could do to keep my eyes on the road."

"Tell me about it. The forests and mountains take your breath away." That's how she'd felt, too, every mile more gorgeous than the last.

"And the wildlife! I saw elk, deer, what I think was a brown bear, a cougar and a moose." Maryann brightened, as if she had truly enjoyed the experience. "It was the moose's fault I missed the turnoff sign to Treasure Creek. It's not like an urban area. There was only one road sign, so I kept driving north."

"You turned right around, didn't you?"

"No. I didn't realize I was off-course until I came to this tiny town and stopped for gas. I'd driven most of an entire day in the wrong direction. I was mesmerized by the mountain range. I can see why you want to stay."

"Really? You're serious? Stay with me. You can share my room."

"I see that smile. You think I'm really here because of the magazine article. You couldn't be more wrong. I'm here to knock some sense into that head of yours if I have to."

"What about dragging me back home?"

"That part I might be willing to compromise on. It really is lovely country, and I've met the nicest people here."

"Oh, I know." That was the reason she had to stay— for one person in particular. She could tell Maryann was about to bring the conversation back around to Gage. Steadfast love for him burned in her heart, a love so strong and deep she'd never known the likes of it before.

"You must be Karenna." A petite woman with wavy, shoulder-length hair approached them. "Gage has told me all about the new nanny he hired for Matthew. Hi, Matthew."

"Oh!" The baby clapped his hands, beaming.

"I'm Karenna." Who exactly was this very pretty woman who knew Gage so well? She was surprised at the protectiveness that leaped to life within her. "How do you know Matthew?"

Then it occurred to her, this was a close-knit town. Every local probably knew about Gage's situation with his nephew.

"I'm his boss." The woman's smile was friendly and open.

"You're Amy James." The pieces clicked into place in Karenna's brain. She noticed the two small boys clinging to each of their mother's hands. "I've heard so much about you, it's like I already know you."

"Likewise. Well, the truth is, Gage isn't much of a talker, but I was able to read between the lines. I'm so glad to meet you. This is Sammy. This is Dexter." Amy swung one hand and then the other. "It's a blessing to Gage to have a nanny for Matthew. He's a tough guy on the outside, but not on the inside."

"So I've discovered." Her thoughts boomeranged to Gage. He'd been more than distant and more than worried. Had he figured out she was in love with him? Had her level of esteem for him accidentally shown on her face?

Amy and Maryann were talking, and the words made no sense. They rattled around in her head, as if her skull had become a cavern. Empty, she could only stare in the direction Gage had gone. Maybe there was more to his pulling back. Maybe she had been too transparent. What if he had figured out how she felt? Then that meant he wasn't happy about it.

Fine, that wasn't a surprise. He had been very clear on his opinion about serious relationships. But he'd been icy and abrupt. He didn't want her. He didn't love her. And she feared the next time they met, he wouldn't hesitate to tell her so.

How was she going to face him?

"I never thought I would see the day," Amy was saying. "Gage has been closed off since his divorce. I know he's lonely, but he won't reach out to anyone."

"And you're telling me he's in love with Karenna?" Maryann asked. "Karenna already feels the same way about him."

"Maryann!" Did her cousin need to be blunt?

"What? You might not have said it, but I read between the lines. Besides, you are a soft touch. Alan wasn't good enough for you, in my opinion, and I'm not sure this Gage is, either."

"You will be, once you get to know him." Defensive, she drew herself up full height. She was dying inside, but it wasn't Gage's fault. "He's a good man, that's all I'm saying. Will the two of you stop looking at me like that?"

"It's all right if you're not ready," Amy said, kindly. "We don't have to mention this again, but that isn't going to stop us from being friends."

"Good, I would like that." It was impossible not to like Amy James. Her two little boys stood at her side, watching with wide gray eyes. What cuties.

"We're treasure hunters," the youngest informed her, with great earnestness.

"*Secret* treasure hunters," the oldest boy added. "We're not supposed to tell anyone we found the map."

"They have been playing treasure hunter all morning." Amy winced, and she let go of Dexter's hand to rest her free hand on her purse. "I had better get them something to eat."

"The barbecue smells good." Karenna smiled at the boys. "It's been a pleasure meeting you, Amy."

"The pleasure was all mine," Amy said warmly. "Why don't both of you come over to my house on Monday at six? I'll fix supper and introduce you around. We will have a wonderful time."

"I would like that." And it was true. Karenna found herself smiling. She fit in here. Being in Treasure Creek felt right. She wanted it to be a part of her life.

"I'll look forward to it," Maryann said, shifting Matthew onto her other hip.

"Great." Amy herded her sons into the shade of the church, where the reverend was manning the barbecue.

"Isn't she nice? I'm having such a good time," Maryann announced. "I'm so glad I came."

"Me, too." Karenna wrapped her cousin into another hug. How good it was to have her here. "I'm getting hungry, too."

"Let's go find out what exactly they are barbecuing. Come on."

"What do you say, Matthew?" Karenna asked.

"Eee!" The boy agreed, enthusiastically.

The sky was a cloudless blue, the merry notes of conversation and laughter carried on the wind. There was no reason not to be happy. As she and Maryann made their way to the dessert table, all Karenna could think about was Gage.

* * *

What passed for nightfall in Alaska this time of year drained the last of the light from the sky, casting the forested slopes of the mountains in fathomless shadows. Strapped into a jump seat with a pair of binoculars in hand, Gage hadn't expected Tucker's downed plane would have been found quickly, but he held out hope anyway. He'd been on enough searches to know they didn't always end happily. Many had ended in the worst possible way.

Please, not this time, he prayed. The late-night skies felt desolate, and although he was high in the air, and therefore closer to God physically, he didn't feel closer emotionally. He'd been shut down so long, he didn't know if he would ever be able to believe in faith and love again.

And that led him right back to the woman he'd been fighting to keep out of his thoughts. Karenna. Loving her was only going to end badly, he knew for a fact and from personal experience. He'd tried the happily-ever-after route and he'd failed miserably. He hadn't been enough for one woman, how could he be able to trust another to stay with him through thick and thin?

"We've got to head back to camp." Reed's voice came over the headphones. "It's too dark."

"I'm not giving up," Jake, across the aisle in the other jump seat, ground out, adamant. "Tucker is my friend. I won't leave him out there."

"We have to," Reed explained. "It's too dangerous for the pilot. We can start again at first light."

"It will be all right," Gage assured Jake. "We'll find Tucker."

But alive, or dead? That he couldn't say. Judging by his silence, Jake knew it, too. Not another word was spoken as the helicopter wheeled southward toward home.

Chapter Fourteen

"Karenna! Yoo-hoo!" Jean stood up at the end of a pew in the middle row of the church, waving one arm as high as she could reach. Matthew, tucked in her other arm, blew bubbles happily. "Over here! I saved you and Maryann a spot."

As glad as she was to see Jean, Gage was missing. A cold dread swished through her, leaving her feeling half frozen as she forced her feet down the aisle. She was grateful for Maryann beside her, who waved in return and marched ahead, taking the lead. She only had to follow her cousin to the right pew.

"So wonderful to meet you, Maryann," Jean greeted warmly, in her grandmotherly way. "It's so wonderful to have you here. Karenna and I haven't had much of a chance to talk about her family. Come sit right beside me and tell me everything."

"You want all the scoop on my dear cousin." Maryann seemed to think that was funny. She took charge of the gurgling baby. "There isn't a lot to tell, but I do have a few funny stories from our childhood up my sleeve."

"Do tell," Jean invited, holding out her hand to squeeze Karenna's warmly. "I want to learn everything I can about the girl. I have my reasons."

One look into those merrily twinkling eyes, and Karenna's pulse lurched to a stop. Had Jean already figured out what was going on? Had her feelings been so easy to read that not only Gage had guessed, but Jean, too? Who else had figured out how impossibly deep her love for the man went? She sank onto the end of the bench, numbness filling her.

Gage wasn't here. She knew he was still out searching for his missing friend, because she'd spoken to Jean on the phone earlier in the morning, but his absence felt significant. It felt like a sign of things to come. She could not forget how he'd stalked away from her last night so remote, like a stranger, the emotional bond between them as good as gone.

"You girls have to come join me for dinner tonight." Jean looked more relaxed, and the color in her cheeks was rosy. "I won't take no for an answer. I know the two of you are staying with the Michaelses, but as wonderful as our pastor and his wife are, it's not right for them to monopolize you."

"Dinner sounds wonderful. We're getting so many invitations. It's nice to be popular," Maryann said, laughing when Matthew held out his arms, straining toward Karenna. "I think someone is sweet on you."

"I have that effect on handsome guys." Hard not to love the little boy, who was flashing his merry dimples at her. His gaze searched hers and he laughed, as if certain he was about to have his way. She took him into her arms, cradling him lovingly. She was already far too fond of the Parker family, but that didn't stop her affection. She pressed a kiss to the crown of the boy's downy head and he sighed contentedly, pressing against her with all his might.

"Why, Amy James. Is that you?" Jean asked. "Your boys are looking exceptionally handsome this morning. I hear they are getting into all sorts of trouble."

Karenna glanced over her shoulder, where Amy sat with her adorable little sons. "Hi, Amy."

"Hi Karenna and Maryann." Amy's hand rested lightly on her purse, tucked on the pew beside her. "Yes, my boys keep me on my toes."

"We're huntin' for treasure," Dexter explained. "It's real hard work."

"I'm helpin'," Sammy piped up.

"That sounds like great fun," Karenna said. "I'm sure you boys are the best prospectors ever."

"Yep," the boys agreed, nodding sweetly.

"Where's Gage?" Amy asked.

"Out on a search-and-rescue." She adjusted Matthew in her arms to make him more comfortable. "A friend of his is missing."

"Yes, Tucker." She brushed a hand over Sammy's hair, smoothing a windblown hair into place. "His plane went down in the storm. I have a call in to Reed. As far as I know, they haven't found him yet."

"How terrible."

"I just heard that several people, including some women, were reported missing this morning," Maryann added. "The last anyone heard, they were going off to find Mack Tanner's buried treasure. Just goes to show, when it comes to a fortune, some folks lose their common sense."

"I guess so." Reed was right, she thought, as Reverend Michaels stepped up to the altar. Even the slightest rumor about the map had caused problems. What should she do? Did she put it back into hiding and forget about it? Or did she chase after the fortune as others were doing, as if money was what mattered? Surely that was not what the Lord intended.

"Good morning, everyone," the kindly reverend greeted, as he opened his Bible. "I'm thankful to see so many of your smiling faces here, faces I already know and others I hope to. Before I begin the opening prayer, I want to say a few words. There's been a lot of speculation about the legend of Mack Tanner and his hidden treasure. I certainly heard a lot about it last evening. It was quite the topic of conversation at our first Meet and Greet. I heard from the police chief this morning that several folks have been reported missing. They went off searching for gold and haven't come back. We pray God is with them and sees them safely home.

"First Timothy tells us, *for the love of money is a root of all kinds of evil, for which some have strayed from the faith in their greediness, and pierced themselves through with many sorrows.* Now I want to ask all of you to forget the rumors circulating about a treasure map. I've heard all kinds of things. Some folks want to steal the map. Others are making a profit from selling fake maps. Even some of you are wondering if Amy James is lying to protect the real fortune in gold. Greed is not the answer, my friends, but trust in the Lord is. Now let us pray."

There was her solution. Amy folded her hands and checked on the boys to make sure they were doing the same. How dear they looked, dressed in white shirts and black trousers, their fingers clasped in prayer. Overwhelmed, she ran a loving hand over each downy head. Love—that was what life was about, not money.

Her great-great-grandfather had loved his neighbors,

his community and his town. He'd been committed to doing business the right way, in helping where he could. Those stories were part of the family legends, too. So she intended to honor his memory by finding the treasure and using it not for herself or her business, but to help the town. The library was in danger of closing. The schools needed new books and building repairs. That treasure, if it existed, could do a world of good for Treasure Creek.

As Reverend Michaels's prayer lifted through the sanctuary, she added one of her own. *Thank You, Father, for guiding me. Now I know what to do.*

In the midday heat in the middle of a mountainous ridge, Gage swiped the sweat trickling into his eyes and called a break. The word echoed down the line, as the six-man team he'd assembled to walk the deep ravines and pockets on the mountainside collapsed onto rocks, logs or the bare ground, and dug water bottles out of their packs.

"This is slow going." Jake ambled over, nursing a slight limp, water in hand.

"We're making good progress, trust me." Gage twisted the cap on his bottle and drank deep. "It was good of you to use your own money for the search."

"What's the point of having it, if you can't help your friends?" Although Jake was a millionaire because his family was in the oil business, he was hiking up the mountainside right along with the rest of the extra men he'd hired. "I have a bad feeling about this, Gage. What if he's hurt and we can't find him in time?"

"We're doing all we humanly can. Thanks to you, we've got twice the usual number of birds in the sky, searching his possible flight path. We've got eyes on the ground looking for the wreckage." It had been a tough day, and it wasn't over yet. "Get off your feet for a few minutes. Take care of that blister."

"Will do." Jake ambled away, resolute.

Gage took his own advice. He spied a log in the shade and settled onto it. What was Karenna doing right now? Was she catching up with her cousin? Or had Bucky asked her out on a date yet?

Anguish hit him like a falling meteor. He reeled, surprised at the depth of his feelings. That was a mighty strong reaction about a woman he wasn't in love with.

You don't love her, he told himself. But he knew it was no longer true.

The dreamy evening light filtered through the tall evergreens and onto Gage's back deck. Karenna set the iced-tea pitcher on the edge of the table. A restful breeze whispered through the boughs and stirred the fragrance from the blooming roses.

"You have a lovely home, Jean." Maryann settled Matthew into his high chair. "It's like paradise here. After church, Karenna and I went for a long drive. Every view we came across was spectacular."

"We are blessed living here." Jean eased into a chair. "It's a great lifestyle. Not as full of entertainment and variety like you have in California, I expect."

"No, but I can see trading malls and cineplexes for this." Maryann appeared relaxed, as if the fresh air and the inspiring views had deeply affected her. "I imagine jobs aren't too plentiful here."

"No, but things are picking up." Jean patted the empty seat beside here. "Karenna, come sit. You have waited on me enough. Maryann, do you know she made the spaghetti?"

"Is this Grandma Olive's meatball recipe?" Her cousin didn't miss much, and the unspoken thought was on her face. The special meatball recipe. The one their grandma had made, which had prompted their grandfather to propose.

"It is," she confessed, cringing. Maryann would read way too much into it. The last thing she wanted was for Jean to know—that is, if she hadn't guessed already. She hadn't been trying to get Gage's attention with her cooking. "That wasn't why I made it. I wanted to make a good impression, is all."

"It's a fine recipe," Jean chimed in. "I've never tasted better. Shall I say the grace?"

"Please." Karenna took a seat, bowed her head and hoped, when the blessing was done, she could steer the conversation away from any mention of Gage.

"Dear Lord," Jean began. "Please watch over our friend Tucker Lawson and see him safely home. As Reverend Michaels reminded us in church today, the true riches in life are the things we cannot buy. We are grateful for Your gifts of love and life and friendship. Please keep us ever mindful of their value in our lives. Amen."

"Amen." Karenna didn't dare look across the table. She feared Jean had already guessed. The last thing she wanted was her affections for her hunky grandson to be dinner conversation. "Would you like some bread, Maryann?"

"I should say no, but I won't." Her cousin took the basket and added several buttery slices of French bread to her plate. "Thank you for making me feel right at home, Jean."

"Nonsense. Karenna's family is our family." The

older woman did seem overly pleased as she dished up her plate.

"Eeee!" Matthew agreed, smacking the flat of his hand on his tray and scattering a few pieces of cereal.

"He agrees." Jean looked triumphant.

Apparently, her secret was not so secret. Mortified, she searched for a safe topic. Before she could find one, a rumbling engine broke the evening's stillness. Gravel crunched beneath tires as Gage's Jeep rolled into sight. The man behind the wheel was grim and spent. His door creaked open, and his gait rang heavy and weary. A few tears marked the shirt he wore, his jeans were covered with dust and dirt and grime ran in rivulets down his face and neck.

Poor Gage. Defeat darkened him as he hiked onto the deck.

"Don't say it." Jean bowed her head. "I've been praying for that lad."

"No news yet. We're clinging to hope." He didn't sound as if that were true. He looked short on any kind of hope. Maybe exhaustion was the reason he avoided eye contact with her, although he did glance in Jean's and Maryann's direction. "Go ahead and eat. I'll dish up later."

She wanted to comfort him. She longed for the right to go to his side and hold him until his sorrows eased. It was torture to sit and do nothing. Shadows followed him and she wanted to be the one to chase them away.

"Go to him," Jean urged. "He needs you."

"No, he doesn't need me." He couldn't even look at her. What if he was rejecting her in subtle, small ways? Something had changed, she was certain of it.

"He needs a meal. Go make a plate for him. I warmed

up the entire pan of spaghetti. It's on the stove." Jean's request was a sincere one. "As a favor to me?"

"I can't say no to you." She pushed away from the table. Jean had no idea how difficult it was to face Gage. To walk through the door and pretend that she wasn't breaking apart inside. To pretend that even the idea of Gage's rejection didn't bring her to her knees.

She found him in the living room, sitting on one end of the couch with his face in his hands. A perfect silhouette of despair. "Gage?"

He didn't move.

"I can see the search isn't going well." She eased onto the cushion beside him. "I'm sorry for your friend."

"The statistics are against him. Most people don't survive a small-plane crash. Add to that the terrain and the trees. Wildlife. No one saw him go down. There were no houses around. No roads. If he did manage to survive but was injured, every hour we don't find him…" He didn't finish. A muscle jumped in his jaw.

"We all have been praying for him."

"For all the good that's done."

"If prayer can't make a difference, then nothing can." Couldn't he see that? Or had he gone so far he could never find his way back to faith?

"I know you're right. It just doesn't feel that way." He straightened up, exhaustion weighing on him. "How do you do it? You are the most optimistic person I know. When your wedding plans fall apart, you forge ahead and start a new life. When a man you've devoted seven years to abandons you, you don't let it stop you."

"You make me sound like something I'm not. I'm trying to do my best to go on, not to fall back."

"I wish I could be more like you." He wanted to pull her into his arms and soak in her goodness. He wished his doubts would vanish and he could be the man he used to be. One who laughed and loved and believed.

The sound of an approaching engine interrupted him, stopping the words that were on his lips, the ones meant to drive her away forever. Best left for another time, he decided as he stood to get a good look at the vehicle trundling down the lane. A white SUV. He couldn't believe his eyes. He felt as if his world ended as the driver's door swung open.

"Who is that?" Karenna joined him at the window, caring and comforting. "I hope it isn't bad news about your friend."

"No, they would have called." This was something else entirely. Another wounded relationship he hadn't been able to fix. "The prodigal brother has returned."

"You mean Matthew's father?"

"Yes." Typical. Whatever the reason had brought Ryan back, Gage couldn't stomach it, not after spending the day searching for Tucker and fearing for his death. He was ripped apart over Karenna. Why now, he wondered as he stormed through the house. Why did Ryan have to come back when the baby was happy again? When Gage had finally let himself care?

"Hey, bro!" Ryan called, as he climbed out of his rig. He strutted into sight as if he didn't have a care in the world. "You don't look so good."

"I've been out on a search." Wasn't he obvious? He didn't feel particularly charitable toward his brother. He fisted his hands, holding them rigid to his sides, so he wasn't tempted to act out of hurt and an anger he didn't understand. How could his brother stroll back into their lives as if he'd done nothing wrong?

"Ryan!" Gran rushed down the steps and threw herself into Ryan's arms. Her voice warbled with tears.

"You are a sight for sore eyes, my boy. To think, I have been worried sick over you."

"You have? What for?" He jingled his car keys with one hand. "Wait, I know. I'm a few days late. Knowing you, you got to worrying if I would keep my word."

"What word?" Gage ground out. They hadn't spoken in six months.

"That I would be gone two weeks. Three tops."

"When did you say that?" Typical Ryan. Good natured, good intentioned, but he fell down on the follow-through. Out of the corner of his eye, he noticed Karenna on the deck cradling the baby. Her nearness made it hard to concentrate. "You never said it to me or Gran."

"Didn't you get my note? Oh, man, I can't believe it. Maybe it blew away. I left a letter with Matthew. I was running late for the airport, so I hit the doorbell and drove off."

"You left a baby on the doorstep." Gage growled. "We thought the worst."

"That I wasn't coming back? Why would I do something so dumb? I love my son. You know that. He's why I had to go."

"Go where?"

"I flew down to Portland."

"To party?" Gage asked.

"No, you blockhead. Matthew needs a mother, don't you think? I joined one of those dating services online and wanted to meet this girl. She was just what I was looking for."

"You went to meet a girl?" Gran locked her hands together as if in prayer. "Glory sakes, this is great news. Ryan, you are going to buckle down now, and raise this child the right way?"

"That's what I've been trying to do. It didn't work out." Ryan glanced around, turning on his charm like a switch. "There's my boy. And who are these beautiful women on your deck?"

Matthew's squeals filled the silence, a rather awkward one. Ryan had come to take the baby. That meant Gage no longer needed a nanny. He no longer needed Karenna.

Not true. What he felt was a whole other type of need, as if he were blind and required her in order to see. That wasn't what he wanted, not at all. He straightened his shoulders, a warrior preparing for battle.

"I'm Maryann," the cousin spoke up. "Karenna has been caring for Matthew in your absence."

"Gage, you didn't need to hire a sitter." Ryan lifted his son from Karenna's arms, and his tone softened. "But I appreciate everything you have done for my son."

"It was my pleasure. He's a good, sweet baby." Matthew squealed again, apparently glad to see his daddy. He held on tight to Ryan's shirt with both little fists.

A tearing sensation ripped through him, and Gage had to look away. The boy would leave with his brother, no doubt, and that would be that. The argument between them remained. Neither of them had changed. Ryan was still ducking responsibility and Gage was never going to approve of it.

A weight like a thousand-pound boulder settled on his chest. Karenna would be going, too.

"Amy James left a message on my voicemail about having work for me." Ryan kissed Matthew's forehead and carried him to the patio table. "I've interrupted supper. I'm sorry. Sit back down or the food will get cold."

"Then you will be staying in town?" Gran's gait livened as she took her chair. "You could find an apartment nearby, so I could see my great-grandson as often as I please."

"That sounds like a good plan to me." Ryan held up his hand as Gran tried to hand him her plate. "No, you eat. I already grabbed a bite in town."

There was something different about his little brother, something Gage couldn't name. They hadn't spoken for six months. It was hard to do it now, so he didn't ask. But he hoped. Maybe Ryan really was turning his life around.

"Nice to see you again." He flashed a winning smile at Maryann.

Maryann laid her napkin in her lap, eyeing Ryan as if she were perfectly aware he was a charmer, and hardly approved.

"Did you both read about Treasure Creek in that magazine article?" Ryan asked amicably. "Is that why you're here?"

"I was the one who read it, and then Maryann decided to join me." Karenna's cheer was forced.

Gage reckoned only he could recognize it. He noticed the strain around her eyes and her unhappiness beneath the surface.

So she had realized it, too. Their time together was coming to a quick close.

"I can't believe all the women in town." Ryan leaned his cheek gently against the crown of his son's head, as if savoring the feel of holding him again. "It's the reason I left Treasure Creek. No women."

"I thought it was because you were furious at me." Gage propped his shoulder against the side of the house, keeping himself apart from the group, needing to be distant.

"Face it, bro. You're usually mad at me. That's no reason for me to run off."

"I suppose the partying was better in Portland?"

"Those days are gone. You know I was hurting after Wendy died. I acted out in ways I regret. But if there's one thing this trip to Oregon taught me, it's how much I love my boy. I could barely breathe without him."

"Oh!" Matthew added, as if he were glad to be in his daddy's arms, too.

Gage took one long last look at Karenna, steeled himself and disappeared into the house. He'd had enough for one day. He went upstairs to shower. When he came back downstairs, she was waiting for him. Alone.

Chapter Fifteen

The moment of truth. Karenna set her chin, gathered every last shred of her dignity and faced the man ambling toward her in the waning daylight. Freshly showered, with his damp hair dark against his face and wearing an old T and shorts, his bare feet whispered against the deck. Her pulse skidded painfully, but she didn't run.

"I wanted to say goodbye, since there's no reason for me to come tomorrow. You no longer need a nanny." She sounded croaky, but other than that he might not know she was dying inside.

"I'm going to miss the little guy," he said.

And I'm going to miss you. She prayed that sentiment did not show on her face, because she already knew other emotions had, which was the very reason Gage kept his eyes averted as he pulled a chair from the table and swung it a good distance from her before he folded his big frame into it.

"You're his uncle. It's not as if you can't hang out with him. It sounds as if Ryan will be able to get his old job back with the tour company, so he will be nearby."

"That won't matter. Tonight was the most we've spoken since a few weeks after Matthew was born."

"What happened?"

"We had a big blowup." Enough said, he figured, intending to change the topic back to what remained unspoken between them.

"What did you argue about?" she asked, before he could divert her.

"At first, we argued because I thought he should marry Matthew's mother."

"Did I hear you right?"

"I know. You never would have pictured me endorsing marriage, huh?"

"I thought you were strictly against the institution."

"I'm more like anti-trust. A woman you can trust is rare. Add that to the fact I don't trust easy after what happened with Margaret, and I don't see how anyone can say 'I do'." He hated to do it, but he had to let her know what he was. When he did, she was going to walk away and never look back. "But there are reasons to marry, and giving a child a stable home to grow up in is one of them."

"So you advised Ryan to marry for duty's sake?"

"I believe I told him that it would be like hurling himself off the edge of a cliff and crashing on the rocks below, but he ought to do it for his son's sake."

"Oh, Gage." Her disappointment in him felt like a blow, but it didn't diminish the glow of love revealed in her eyes.

Love for him. He bowed his head. "Two days later Matthew was born, and Wendy was gone. Ryan blamed me. He said my attitude about marriage made him afraid to commit. When he was ready to marry her, it was too late."

There, now she knew the truth.

"That's what you think about marriage?"

"Yes, and it's not going to change." He watched realization dawn on her face, and he hated himself for the sadness moving into the perfect blue of her eyes. Sorrow hooked deep, and he could not tell if it was his or hers that he felt. He gathered his strength to land the final blow. "I can't be the man you need."

"I know. You have been honest about that all along." Her chin lifted a notch. For all her frailness and sweetness, she was stronger than any woman he'd ever known. She did not betray a single emotion as she rose from the chair. "I think you should ask Ryan to move into the garage apartment, so that you two can become closer again."

"The apartment. I hadn't even thought about it. You should still have it."

"It wouldn't be right for me to take it." She hooked her purse over her shoulder, wishing her fingers weren't trembling. "I suppose I will see you around town from time to time."

"My grandmother is going to be so disappointed. She adored having you around."

"Jean and I will stay friends." She forced her feet to shuffle forward one step and then another. "We have made plans to meet this week."

"Good. What about your check?"

"You can mail it to Reverend Michaels. He'll make sure I get it." Another step took her farther away from him, the direction the rest of her life would take. Inside, she was shattering, but she straightened her shoulders and forced the pain from her voice. "Perhaps I could use you for a job reference?"

"Sure. I know Amy is hiring. The office has a lot

more paperwork to go with the increased business. You might want to check with her."

"I will. Thanks." Devastation came quietly as she took measured, dignified steps across the gravel. Immeasurable pain crashed through her. This was it. Her final goodbye. "Knowing you has been a privilege."

"No, the privilege was all mine," he corrected, his voice coming from the darkness now. There was no emotion, no connection, no closeness between them. "Good night, Karenna."

"Bye." She turned her back, unable to watch how easily he could let her go. She wrenched open her car door and wished she could do the same.

Misery tailed him through the kitchen door. It held on with sharp teeth, refusing to let go as he squinted through the reflection in the glass. The Fiat's taillights disappeared, and still he watched. He wished she would come back. Impossible, but he wanted her to come back.

"I never thought I would see the day." Ryan thunked a glass of juice against the countertop.

"What were you doing? Watching me?"

"Yeah, watching you make a fool of yourself."

"What are you talking about?" he barked, doing his best to be the Gage he used to know, the one who felt comfortable scowling and grimacing to keep everyone away, even family. Why wasn't it working now?

"Don't tell me you finally found a woman who will have you, and you let her get away?"

Gage winced. Good thing twilight was falling, because at least he could pretend the agony didn't show. Denial seemed like the way to go. "Don't know what you're talking about. I didn't let her do anything. She got in her car and drove away."

"My mistake." Ryan laughed, almost bitterly. "For a moment there, I really thought you'd fallen for her."

"Me?" He was head over heels, beyond the point of no return.

"You're right. You, the one who told me that love is like being sucked down a dangerous river, pulled under in a rapids and then hurled off a waterfall." He shook his head, looking as if this was all a waste of time. "I should have known. You have a heart of steel."

I wish I didn't. What he wanted was to be a man full of illusions, one who could trust her love would last.

"I've been doing a lot of thinking about the kind of man I want to be," Ryan told him. "I'm getting my life on track. I'm going to work hard to provide for my son. Karenna talked me into going to the singles meeting at the church. I don't want to wind up like you, Gage."

Neither do I. He didn't know what else to say. The day had taken a toll on him. Worn out, he dragged his feet around the corner. Tomorrow was an early a.m. wakeup call and another sixteen-hour shift walking the line, searching for Tucker.

Tomorrow was also the first day of his life without Karenna.

"Gage." Gran looked up from her knitting. "Don't think I didn't hear what you told Ryan. It's been a long time since you and I discussed what happened in Seattle and the bitterness you've been carrying around."

"Not tonight, Gran." Not ever, if he could help it. He passed a hand over his face. He felt like a dead man walking.

"Where do you think you're going?" Her needles clacked as she gave him her best schoolmarm look.

"You stay here and listen. You can walk away when I'm done."

"I told you, Gran—"

"I heard you. It's now or never, boy. I've let you have time, thinking that's what you needed to heal. But I can see now I've been wrong." Worry wreathed her face. Her needles paused in midpurl. "You have to know not every marriage ends up crashed on the rocks. I had a very fine thirty-seven years with your grandfather. Every day was better than the last. Sure, life got tough sometimes, but our love was tougher. The best thing I ever did was marry that man. There, now I've had my say. Go and get some sleep."

He climbed the stairs desolate, but he didn't feel alone. He swore he felt God's presence on the steps ahead of him, leading the way. There might be hope after all. It had been years, but when he closed his bedroom door, he pulled out his Bible and sat down to read.

I can't be the man you need. Gage's confession haunted her on the long drive home. How could she fault him? He had been honest and upfront. He had gently let her know that he didn't love her. He had done everything right and yet, that didn't lessen the impact.

He didn't love her. That was what mattered. That truth tortured her like nothing ever had. The pain of Alan's abandonment was tiny in comparison—a sign of how great her love for Gage had become. She hadn't been aware of how deeply her affection ran until now.

"You look as though you lost your best friend." Maryann rose from one of two wicker chairs on the Michaelses' front porch. She'd driven her own car home, and was waiting with concern on her face. "What happened?"

"He doesn't love me." She collapsed into the second chair, feeling ready to implode. She didn't want to fall apart. There was nowhere else to run, nothing left to do but to handle this.

Just focus on the future, that's what she had to do. She had to find a way of never thinking of Gage again. Maybe then she could put a layer of steel around her heart. If it worked for Gage, then maybe it could work for her.

"I'm sorry." Maryann sounded sincere.

"I would have thought you would be glad. No chance of impulsively getting married now." She meant to sound light and casual, as if Gage's rejection wasn't a big deal.

Total failure.

"Karenna, that's why I came to Alaska. I wanted to keep you from getting hurt."

"It's too late."

"So I see."

Silence fell between them, the understanding, comfortable kind of stillness. Karenna watched the rays of the sun lengthen as it descended in the bay. Shadows crept over the front lawn and finally the porch, as if taking over the world. She felt the darkness fall across her face.

Don't think about Gage and you will be fine. That's what she told herself. Except, she wasn't fine. She wasn't okay. She would never be all right again. Grief battered her, stealing the hope from her soul.

Chapter Sixteen

With a container of cupcakes stacked on the Fiat's passenger seat, Karenna pulled to a stop along the curb in front of Amy's house. She grabbed her purse and the cupcakes. As she hopped out of her car, Maryann pulled up behind her in her rental car.

I can do this, she thought, as she set her chin and pushed misery out of her heart. Life went on. She'd loved and lost before. Of course, losing Alan had been nothing like this, which went to show exactly how much she loved Gage.

She feared she always would. That she would never recover from losing him, her soul mate. Not that she could let anyone aside from Maryann know.

"Are you sure you feel up to this?" Her cousin swung her car door shut, a covered bowl of fruit salad in hand.

"Yes. Life goes on." She lifted her chin a notch, determined to do her best. After all, the only thing broken was her heart.

"Yes, life does go on, but sometimes you take a blow that changes you and you are never the same again."

Maryann's love and kindness showed as they fell into step together. "I'm right here if you need me."

"Thanks." She was blessed to have so much love in her life. She had so very many wonderful blessings. It didn't seem right that the one she couldn't have dimmed the beauty of all the rest. She would somehow find a way to let Gage go. To accept that he was not the love she was meant to spend forever with.

As they headed up the walkway toward the front door, the rise and fall of voices drifted through the screen door. At least something good had already come of the day. Maryann had admitted to falling so far in love with Alaska that she decided to stay the summer. And the day was going to get better with the chance to make new friends. She really did have a lot to be thankful for.

"I'm so glad you two could make it." Amy spotted her before they could step foot on the porch. She opened the door with a smile. "Come in."

"We couldn't resist bringing a contribution," Maryann explained.

"Yes, we didn't want to come empty-handed." Karenna stepped inside the cozy living room and spotted a woman with short brown hair and beautiful blue eyes, at a kitchen table looking defeated. A magazine was open on the tablecloth in front of her. "Hi."

"Hi, there."

"I smell chocolate icing." Amy led the way into the cheerful kitchen. "You didn't have to bring anything, but I'm so glad you did. That smells wonderful."

"I love to bake, I was in the mood for chocolate, and I thought your sons might like some, too." She set the plastic container on the edge of a very tidy counter.

"And I brought a fruit salad to balance all the sugar."

Maryann set down her bowl next to the cupcakes, with a smile.

"I feel healthier already," Amy commented, looking pleased. "I'm sure the boys will be thrilled. Come, sit down. Let me pour you some tea. Do you know Casey Donner? She's one of our tour guides."

"It's nice to meet you." Karenna settled into a chair across from the woman, who looked to be in her twenties, too. "A tour guide? I think I read about you in the magazine article."

"Yes, I did, too." Maryann took an available chair and settled in. "I remember reading about a woman guide."

"That's me, and I'm in a total funk over this." Casey held up the *Now Woman* issue and began to read. "'And, Alaska's Treasures even has a female tour guide! But, ladies, don't worry about her as competition for the town's hunky men, because everyone says that Casey Donner is just one of the guys!' Thanks. That makes me feel so much better."

"I think they meant it as a compliment," Amy said, as she poured tall glasses of sweet tea.

"That's putting a positive spin on it." Casey sighed and closed the magazine. "It's sad that there's nothing feminine at all about me. It's true. I feel like a fool when I wear a dress. Maybe for my ten-year high-school reunion next month I'll wear overalls. What do you think?"

Karenna laughed. She liked Casey. Women with freckles had to stick together. "I think you should be yourself. You have sparkle, Casey. You're fine just the way you are."

"Why, thank you." She took a sip of her glass of tea. "Do we get any of those cupcakes, Amy?"

"We'll have them after we eat. Hold your horses." Amy's laughter sounded light and true as she set the glasses on the table. "I'm going to let the boys eat outside."

"I can hear them." Delighted, Karenna leaned back in her chair. Through the back screen door, she had a clear view of them in their fenced yard, trowels in hand, prospecting in a petunia bed. They played together, as safe and happy as could be.

"I've already got their meal packed up for them, just like real treasure hunters." True love shone through, as Amy gestured toward two small, brown paper sacks on the counter, which had obviously been carefully and lovingly packed. "Casey and I got to thinking that we could make this an impromptu Bible study, if you want."

"That would be great," Karenna smiled.

"Except I left my Bible at the Michaelses'," Maryann pointed out.

"We'll share." Amy slid two juice boxes onto the counter next to the lunch sacks and turned around, spotting an old rolltop desk in the next room. "I think I can find Ben's Bible. I haven't been in it much since he passed."

"Let me go through it," Casey spoke up, clearly a good friend.

"Thanks, but I can do it." Amy lifted her chin, the pain of her loss visible on her lovely face.

Gage wasn't gone. He was still here on earth. Karenna took a shaky breath, realizing the truth at last. She had no right to grieve. He was only gone to her, unlike poor Amy, who had lost her husband tragically.

"Here it is." Amy plucked a well-worn black volume from the top desk, and then her face fell. "What is this?"

"What's what?" Casey pushed out of her chair, crossing the room with a quiet grace and true concern.

"It's a letter from Ben." Amy looked shell-shocked. "It's a letter he wrote to me before he died."

"Let me see." Casey sidled up to her and their heads bent together over the single piece of stationary. Silence descended while they read. Tears filled Amy's eyes and streamed down her face.

"Oh, that's beautiful." Casey sniffled. "Ben truly loved you, Amy."

"I truly loved him." She rubbed at her tears, looking self-conscious, aware how vulnerable she looked. "You all might as well read it, too. It's the only way you will know my Ben."

Karenna took the letter, touched that Amy would share with her and Maryann. They leaned together to read the thoughtfully penned note.

My Dear Amy,
It's late and my gear is packed and ready for another river rapids tour in the morning. I've tried sleeping but I couldn't settle. You were sound asleep, as beautiful as an angel, and I couldn't stand the thought I might wake you, so here I am writing to you from my desk. The need to let you know I love you is so strong, it is a physical pain.

      Maybe I'm more tired than I realize, but I'm reminded of a story my grandmother told me when I was very young. She spoke of my grandfather, who had moved heaven and earth to get a call in to her before his ship left port to fight in the South Pacific. He died on that tour. He'd told my grandmother he felt a yearning from the bottom of his soul to express his love for her. Tonight, that's the yearning I have, too.

I love you, Amy. If something happens to me tomorrow on the river, know this. However much you love me, I love you more. I will always love you. Not even death can diminish it, weaken it or end it. But I want you to be happy. Live the life God has given you. Don't hold back, even for me. The greatest gift you can give me is to find love again. Don't spend Christmas alone. The boys need a father, and you are too special to live your life without love.

Tears blurred the world around her, and she blinked them back, awash in emotion. The letter in her hand was proof that true love mattered. That she and Gage still had a chance for happiness—a rare chance, one that should not be wasted. The sun shone brighter as it tumbled through the windows, a clear sign from above that, finally, she understood what God had been trying to show her all along.

It had been a tough, tough day. Disheartened, Gage took the country lane too fast, his Jeep bouncing in protest whenever it hit a new pothole. His vision threatened to blur from exhaustion—he'd pulled another tough and disappointing shift, and they were no closer to finding Tucker. An hour ago, he'd been rotated out of the team for a mandatory break. He'd fought it, but in the end, it wasn't his say.

All he wanted to do was to find Tucker. He'd gone on a lot of rescues and manned numerous searches over his years of service, but he had a bad feeling. No one wanted to say it, because Tucker was one of their own. Tucker was a good man and a good friend.

"It's too personal for you, Gage." That's what Reed had told him. "You're losing perspective. You're the best we have on the team, but you're no good to me like this. You're no good to Tucker. Go home, get some rest—and some perspective."

Reed was right. Gage's grip on the steering wheel tightened. White knuckled, he stopped for a doe near the roadside. The delicate creature startled, leaping across the pavement with two spotted fawns at her side. The mother and twins bounded away through the brush, disappearing.

Life could be a flecting thing, and the road through it a hard one. As he put his foot on the gas, he thought of the burdens heavy on his shoulders. Ben's death, Matthew's mother's passing, and now Tucker's disappearance. He had to be honest about that. The chances of finding his old friend alive were close to nil. This wasn't the first missing plane he'd searched for. Not once had he found anyone alive.

Defeat battered him as he pulled onto the narrow country lane. Home wouldn't feel like a refuge. He didn't think he could escape from the disillusion he'd been carrying around for so long. They'd all come crashing back the moment Karenna had driven away for a final time. Now they pummeled him worse than before because his hope was gone. Every last drop. Karenna had taken that with her, right along with his heart and, most likely, his soul.

You don't love her, he thought stubbornly, wanting the impossible to be true. *You don't believe in love.*

He felt broken without her. Nothing was the same. She was like a fairy-tale princess who walked into a man's life, changed it and changed him. She made him want to believe in happy endings.

He wanted one with all of his might. But how? How did a man go from disbelief to absolute trust?

Was that her old purple Fiat up ahead? He blinked, trying to focus. Sure enough, her sports car sat parked on the narrow shoulder of the country lane. He had to be imagining it. That couldn't be Karenna. He blinked again and her car was still there. His palms went damp and his pulse thudded to a stop.

What was she doing here? Was something wrong? Or had her car broken down again? He pulled to a stop behind her, his knees shaking as his boots touched the ground. Her car door swung open and she popped into the road like a vision. The sunlight arrowing through the trees found her, highlighting the pure gold in her bouncy hair and accenting the porcelain beauty of her face. She looked like a dream in a simple pink blouse, blue jeans and black boots.

She was his dream.

"Shh!" She put a finger to her lips, a fairy-tale princess in a forest where good prevailed and all endings were happy ones. The wind breezed against her, tossing her hair against the curve of her face, and her beautiful gaze caught him like a trap. "Stay quiet."

"What are you doing here?" he demanded, in a low tone, as he padded toward her. "And why are we whispering?"

"Look." She peered over the roof of her car into the forest.

Cedars reached for the sky, providing a green canopy with glimpses of sun and sky. Birds called from the boughs above and flitted from tree to tree. They were not alone in the woods. He heard a slight rustling and saw a fragile deer watching them with big, brown eyes, spotted fawns at her side.

"It's like a sign," she whispered.

"There are plenty of does and their babies around. I think I just saw that family a few minutes ago, or one just like it. It's not a sign."

"It is when you've been praying for one." She could not take her eyes from the sight. "Aren't they amazing? So beautiful and delicate. Nothing in God's world should be taken for granted."

"That's true. I can't argue with that."

"Finally. That's a miracle in itself."

"Hey." He appeared to be losing his battle to remain stoic and disagreeable. He splayed one hand against the roof of her car and shook his head. "I'm not that bad."

"No, you aren't." When she looked at him, she saw a man who'd learned how to barricade his heart so no more hurt could get in. The problem was, nothing else could. "But you're not so good, either."

"I can't believe a few minutes ago I was almost glad to see you." Dimples teased the corners of his mouth.

"You're going to have to get used to seeing me." She wasn't one to let opportunity pass her by. She certainly did not intend to let the best man in Alaska slip away from her. She'd spent seven years not marrying Alan, and maybe that was for a reason. She'd never been truly sure and eager to take the step. She'd accepted his excuses to put off their wedding. Now she knew what she'd felt for him had been friendship and the longing for true love.

The thing about true love was this: you could pray for it, do your best to find it and try to transform a comfortable relationship into it. But in the end, you couldn't manufacture it. It was a gift from God. A rare blessing given by God at His discretion. Rare enough to fight for.

"I've decided I am going to rent your garage apartment if Ryan doesn't want it." She gathered her courage and laid her hand on his. "I'm fond of Jean and Matthew, so it will be a good situation for me."

"And what about me?"

"I'm certainly not fond of you at all." She sparkled up at him, wondering if he would guess the truth. Did he feel this way, too, as if he were so full of love he could defy gravity and float all the way up to the sky?

"Not fond of me? How can you say that?" He scowled at her, but the gruffness didn't reach his eyes. It didn't dampen the note of affection in his voice. "I hired you when you didn't have a job. I painted the apartment the colors you wanted."

"And those two small gestures are supposed to win my lifelong devotion?" She arched one eyebrow at him, her hand on his, a welcome comfort he could not deny. Amusement flirted in the corners of her mouth as she appeared to battle them down. "I'm going to need something bigger."

"Bigger?"

"This *is* lifelong devotion we're talking about."

"Don't tell me you're one of those marriage-minded women desperate for a husband." Could she feel the tiny tremors shaking him? Did she know how her love was changing him?

For the first time, he imagined a future with her. A wedding with lots of flowers, and her parading down the aisle in a lacy white gown and pure love glowing in her eyes. Fixing suppers in the kitchen together, talking over their day; laughter-filled weekends and quiet moments where their hearts did the talking and no words were needed.

He didn't need to close his eyes to see the family they would have one day. The thought of Karenna cradling their baby brought tears to his eyes. Every last wall fell. Every last piece of doubt tumbled to the ground, irrevocably shattered.

She had changed him. Loving Karenna had brought him back to his heart. Hope took root inside him. Real hope, where none had grown for so long.

"I'm not desperate for just any husband." She bit her bottom lip, as if nervous, and the plea on her dear face was one his soul could hear.

"You have someone in mind?" he asked, although he had a clue.

"Perhaps." Vulnerable, she gazed up at him. Her hand on his trembled, too.

An answering love beat in his heart, one as deep and as abiding. Didn't she know that only she mattered? All he wanted to do was to love her until the end of time. She was the one woman strong of spirit and of heart who could really love him. Her illusions about marriage were all the right ones—she believed in forever love, unyielding loyalty and happiness ever after. He knew her well enough to know that she stood for those ideals.

"I love you, Karenna." His dark gaze searched hers, as if willing her to say the same. "Is it too late? Do you think you can love a man like me?"

"I already do," she confessed. "I intend to love you forever."

"Forever. I like the sound of that."

If a kiss could be perfection, then this would be it. She let her eyes drift shut and savored the sweet bliss. Joy burst inside her like the sweetest hymn.

Epilogue

Two weeks later

"Any more hot dogs?" Ryan called out, from the grill. Several folks in the crowd on the backyard patio called out affirmatives.

"How about it?" Gage asked the beautiful blonde at his side. "Still hungry?"

"I'm stuffed. I should make myself useful and start setting out the dessert." With a grin, Karenna bounced off the picnic bench. Her bouncy hair curled at her shoulders, framing a face made more beautiful with the happy glow of love. "I've got all those chocolate cupcakes I baked and decorated in honor of the first backyard barbecue you've hosted in anyone's memory."

"Hey, I'm new and improved. Might as well have a barbecue." He loved that he could make her laugh, a merry trill that made his spirit whole. He grabbed his empty plate and followed her through the crowd.

"Did you two ladies need anything else?" he asked of Casey and Amy, as he passed by.

"Nothing for me, thanks." Casey shook her head.

"This is a great party, Gage." Amy gathered up her sons' empty plates and took off toward the grill, ready for seconds.

Gage noticed Karenna had stopped to speak with Gran. Probably asking if she needed a refill of lemonade. The older lady patted Karenna's hand adoringly, shook her head no, and said something only Karenna could hear. Every time his beloved laughed, his spirit deepened a little bit more. Because of her, he knew that love could heal. It could give a man hope. Love could also be a sweet sanctuary.

He nodded to the occupants of the next table as he rounded the corner. Jake and Reed sat across from Edward Michaels and his wife, engrossed in conversation. Maryann Jenner, Karenna's cousin, sat next to Patti, a woman Ryan had met at the church singles' group. Both women were enjoying Matthew's antics, as he displayed the new sounds he'd mastered at a volume level that made loud seem quiet.

"Follow me." Gage threaded Karenna's fingers through his and led her around the house. The sounds of the party grew distant. The wind danced in the trees and coaxed fragrance from the blooming roses. A hawk circled lazily, far overhead, joined by his mate. The pair sailed like poetry across the fathomless blue and out of sight.

"Are you happy?"

"Blissful." Gage's question surprised her. They had spent every spare moment they could together, although he was still manning an extensive search for his missing friend. For today, he was off, looking relaxed and as happy as she felt. "Why do you ask?"

"Your happiness has been on my mind a great deal lately." With the roses as his witness, and the sunshine gracing him, he knelt in front of her, his hand tightening on hers. "You came into my life and changed it, Karenna. When I had run out of hope, you showed me buckets of it. When I had lost sight of the good in his world, you gave me a reason to believe."

Her pulse roared to a stop. Was he really kneeling before her? Was this real and not a dream?

"When I thought love was fiction, you convinced me it is the best kind of story come true. I believe in you, Karenna. I believe I can make you happy forever. Please give me the chance. I love you as deep as my heart can go and as strong as my soul can be. Will you marry me?"

"Yes." She loved him more than there were stars in the Alaska sky, and deeper than the vast, blue overhead could reach. She stared at the perfect diamond ring he slipped on her finger, a symbol of his steadfast love. Happiness overwhelmed her. She could see their future together, happily married as man and wife. Cooking dinner, hosting barbecues for friends, helping Jean with the weeding. There would be children one day—a little boy and a little girl, whose laughter would carry on the winds as they raced in this yard.

She simply could not wait to marry him. From this moment on, Gage was her center, her life and her everything. He was her most precious prayer come true. "How does October first sound?"

"Like the start of our happily ever after. And it will be happy. You have my word on that." He drew her into his strong arms and sealed his promise with a kiss.

* * * * *

*For more Treasure Creek,
look for Casey and Jacob's story,
TREASURE CREEK DAD
by Terri Reed,
available in August
from Love Inspired.*

Dear Reader,

Thank you for visiting Treasure Creek, Alaska. I am so
pleased to be a small part of this great series. I hope you
enjoyed coming along with Karenna Digby on her trip
to Alaska, and that you fell in love with this small town
and great characters. There's Amy James, who owns the
Alaska Treasures Tour Company, Delilah Carrington
and Jolene Jones, who are looking for love the same way
Karenna is. And Gage Parker, Klondike search-and-
rescue hero, who just wanted to avoid all the women
swarming into town looking for handsome bachelors.
He didn't believe a single one of them could bring his
embittered heart back to life—not until Karenna showed
him the way to true love and belief. I hope you enjoyed
reading their journey to happily-ever-after as much as
I did writing it.

Thank you for choosing *Klondike Hero*.

Wishing you the best of blessings always,

Jillian Hart

QUESTIONS FOR DISCUSSION

1. At the beginning of the story, how would you describe Karenna's character? What are her weaknesses and strengths? At heart, what are her issues?

2. What is Gage's reaction when he first sees Karenna in her wedding dress? What does this tell you about his character? What are his issues? How have they held him back in living his life?

3. In the beginning of the story Karenna runs from her problems, literally and emotionally. Have you ever felt this way? How does Karenna come to face her problems?

4. Why does Gage hire Karenna? What does this say about him?

5. How would you describe Karenna's faith journey? How does Karenna's faith impact Gage?

6. How would you describe Gage's faith struggles?

7. How does Gage's attitude begin to change toward Karenna through the story? Toward love? Toward marriage?

8. What are the central themes in this romance? How do they develop? What meanings do you find in them?

9. How does God guide both Gage and Karenna through their pain and fears?

10. What role does the community play in the story?

11. What happens to make Gage let go of his past wounds? How does he find self-forgiveness and understanding?

12. When is the moment that Karenna falls in love with Gage? What does she learn about love and life in this story?

13. Have you ever run from love because of past hurts? Were you able to overcome your fears? How?

14. What do you think happens to Karenna's cousin Maryann? Will she stay in Treasure Creek? Fall in love?

15. Would you ever consider making a big move for love? Why or why not?

Love Inspired®

TITLES AVAILABLE NEXT MONTH

Available July 27, 2010

THE DOCTOR'S BLESSING
Brides of Amish Country
Patricia Davids

TREASURE CREEK DAD
Alaskan Bride Rush
Terri Reed

HOMETOWN PROPOSAL
Kellerville
Merrillee Whren

THE COWBOY'S SWEETHEART
Brenda Minton

HOMECOMING HERO
Renee Ryan

WEDDING CAKE WISHES
Wedding Bell Blessings
Dana Corbit

LICNM0710

LARGER-PRINT BOOKS!

GET 2 FREE
LARGER-PRINT NOVELS
PLUS 2 FREE
MYSTERY GIFTS

Love Inspired®

Larger-print novels are now available...

YES! Please send me 2 FREE LARGER-PRINT Love Inspired® novels and my 2 FREE mystery gifts (gifts are worth about $10). After receiving them, if I don't wish to receive any more books, I can return the shipping statement marked "cancel." If I don't cancel, I will receive 6 brand-new novels every month and be billed just $4.74 per book in the U.S. or $5.24 per book in Canada. That's a saving of over 20% off the cover price. It's quite a bargain! Shipping and handling is just 50¢ per book.* I understand that accepting the 2 free books and gifts places me under no obligation to buy anything. I can always return a shipment and cancel at any time. Even if I never buy another book, the two free books and gifts are mine to keep forever.

122/322 IDN E7QP

Name _____ (PLEASE PRINT) _____

Address _____ Apt. # _____

City _____ State/Prov. _____ Zip/Postal Code _____

Signature (if under 18, a parent or guardian must sign) _____

Mail to Steeple Hill Reader Service:
IN U.S.A.: P.O. Box 1867, Buffalo, NY 14240-1867
IN CANADA: P.O. Box 609, Fort Erie, Ontario L2A 5X3

Not valid to current subscribers to Love Inspired Larger-Print books.

**Are you a current subscriber to Love Inspired books
and want to receive the larger-print edition?
Call 1-800-873-8635 or visit www.morefreebooks.com.**

* Terms and prices subject to change without notice. Prices do not include applicable taxes. Sales tax applicable in N.Y. Canadian residents will be charged applicable provincial taxes and GST. Offer not valid in Quebec. This offer is limited to one order per household. All orders subject to approval. Credit or debit balances in a customer's account(s) may be offset by any other outstanding balance owed by or to the customer. Please allow 4 to 6 weeks for delivery. Offer available while quantities last.

Your Privacy: Steeple Hill Books is committed to protecting your privacy. Our Privacy Policy is available online at www.SteepleHill.com or upon request from the Reader Service. From time to time we make our lists of customers available to reputable third parties who may have a product or service of interest to you. If you would prefer we not share your name and address, please check here. ☐

Help us get it right—We strive for accurate, respectful and relevant communications. To clarify or modify your communication preferences, visit us at www.ReaderService.com/consumerschoice.

LILP10R

HARLEQUIN®

A Romance

FOR EVERY MOOD™

Spotlight on

Heart & Home

Heartwarming romances
where love can happen
right when you least expect it.

See the next page to enjoy a sneak peek
from Harlequin® American Romance®,
a Heart and Home series.

Five hunky Texas single fathers—five stories from Cathy Gillen Thacker's LONE STAR DADS *miniseries. Here's an excerpt from the latest, THE MOMMY PROPOSAL from Harlequin American Romance.*

"I hear you work miracles," Nate Hutchinson drawled. Brooke Mitchell had just stepped into his lavishly appointed office in downtown Fort Worth, Texas.

"Sometimes, I do." Brooke smiled and took the sexy financier's hand in hers, shook it briefly.

"Good." Nate looked her straight in the eye. "Because I'm in need of a home makeover—fast. The son of an old friend is coming to live with me."

She was still tingling from the feel of his warm palm. "Temporarily or permanently?"

"If all goes according to plan, I'll adopt Landry by summer's end."

Brooke had heard the founder of Nate Hutchinson Financial Services was eligible, wealthy and generous to a fault. She hadn't known he was in the market for a family, but she supposed she shouldn't be surprised. But Brooke had figured a man as successful and handsome as Nate would want one the old-fashioned way. *Not that this was any of her business…*

"So what's the child like?" she asked crisply, trying not to think how the marine-blue of Nate's dress shirt deepened the hue of his eyes.

"I don't know." Nate took a seat behind his massive antique mahogany desk. He relaxed against the smooth leather of the chair. "I've never met him."

"Yet you've invited this kid to live with you permanently?"

"It's complicated. But I'm sure it's going to be fine."

Obviously Nate Hutchinson knew as little about teenage

boys as he did about decorating. But that wasn't her problem. Finding a way to do the assignment without getting the least bit emotionally involved was.

Find out how a young boy brings Nate and Brooke together in THE MOMMY PROPOSAL, coming August 2010 from Harlequin American Romance.

HAREXP0810

Gage propped his shoulder against the side of the house,